NATALIE-NICOLE BATES

That Winter Touch

The Albion 1892 (Book 5)

Caroline,

Welcome to THE ALBION WORLD!

Hope you enjoy the STORY.

Natalie-Nicole Bates

Natalie-Nicole Bates

Contents

Chapter 1

Next Christmas would be different.

Sam McGreevy would be somebody.

No longer a barman or the man forced to work lonely nights at the front desk of The Albion Hotel for extra money.

Not that there was anything wrong with being a barman.

But next Christmas, he would be a doctor.

A man of respect.

No one would look down on him anymore.

He had his fill of stuck-up rich boys who wore the finest hand-tailored suits every day to class while Sam alternated his meager wardrobe of two medium-quality sack suits that were left behind at the hotel by a guest who never returned to claim their clothing. It was just serendipitous that the suits fit close enough that his sister was able to alter them to fit his body even better.

In truth, he envied the spoiled rich boys who didn't need to worry about working a job because their fathers financed their lifestyles.

It also secretly thrilled him to know several were dumb as tree stumps and certainly would come to find out very soon they failed their final exams.

Of course, spreading a little money around might magically inflate their final exam scores.

The anatomical drawings on the yellowing pages of the anatomy text by candlelight began to swim in his vision.

He was so tired.

Maybe he could just close his eyes and rest for a few minutes. After all, it was quiet at the hotel. All the guests were presumably tucked away in their beds for the night.

What would it hurt?

Sam rested his head awkwardly in the crook of his arm and closed his eyes.

Yes, next Christmas, even sooner, things would be so different.

All the sacrifices would be worth it.

This past year, his days had been spent between the college classrooms and the hospital.

Sometimes it was the prison or the asylums where he would be sent to practice his craft.

Not that he minded.

Sam firmly believed that every person, no matter what their situation in life, deserved adequate medical care.

But the years of spending his days at the medical college, followed by a few blessed hours of sleep, squeezing in study time, and then tending bar at The Albion, followed some nights spent manning the front desk was exacting its toll on him.

He was only twenty-five, but the mirror reflected a much older man with dark circles under his eyes and a perpetual look of tiredness.

Surely now that he finished his studies and final exams had been sat, he could just relax, and dare he think it, *sleep*?

Prepare for a future as a practicing physician.

Perhaps someday a surgeon, or maybe even someday a coroner.

Word was around that the morgue was so busy, the town the coroner, Doctor Anton Larsen, was looking to hire a deputy coroner, maybe more than one.

Of course, to be considered at all he had to have successfully passed all his final exams.

Sam thought it rather cruel of the medical college to not release the results of the final exams until shortly before Christmas day. For those who failed, it would not be a happy Christmas.

Not at all.

Three more weeks or so and he would know if he was Doctor Sam McGreevy, or to remain Sam the barman or Sam the occasional late-night front desk man.

The thought of failing depressed his already tired body and mind.

It wasn't that being a barman was a lowly position in life to hold. No, he liked working at The Albion. It was clean, and warm, good food from the kitchen, and the staff was friendly.

The owner, Thaddeus Anderton was more than a fair man.

Mister Anderton understood Sam's predicament with needing to balance work and college, and even allowed Sam to occupy a room on the men's floor of the hotel without charge.

And Mister Anderton never required him to work in the basement of The Albion.

No one talked openly about the going's on in the basement of the hotel after ten at night. But everyone knew the basement came alive with free-flowing booze, women of a certain reputation, and gambling. It was called a speakeasy. An establishment without the proper licensure now required by the government. Mister Anderton had somewhat of a reputation around Carlyle Street and preferred to bribe and blackmail rather than grovel for an establishment license.

Sam admired Mister Anderton's entrepreneurial spirit and his business savvy which granted him a very comfortable lifestyle.

The familiar creak of the front door of The Albion Hotel opening caused Sam to wake with a jolt.

It had to be past two in the morning, he realized.

Not many check-ins at that hour, but occasionally, a late train pulled into the station.

He quickly got into an upright position, his spine cracked in protest. No one who now entered the hotel would know he had just been fast asleep.

He recognized the coachman who led by the arm, a young woman wrapped up warmly in a coat, and a fancy fur hat to match.

It was an odd sight; coachman didn't generally hold the arm of a young woman.

A much older woman he could assist without raising an eyebrow. Perhaps this young lady was a relative of the coachman who was arriving on Carlyle Street for a spot of Christmas shopping. This time of the year, people came from near and far to shop for the upcoming holiday.

"Good evening, Sam, this young woman has a reservation and is here to meet her auntie."

The coachman swept his free hand across his eyes and shook his head.

Sam caught his meaning immediately.

The young woman was blind.

"Constance, I am going to leave you now with Sam. He will get you checked in to the hotel, and fetch your auntie. I will bring in your bags, and leave them at the check-in desk," the coachman told her.

She turned to the sound of his voice and smiled the most beautiful smile Sam had ever seen.

"Thank you so much for your kindness. I truly appreciate your assistance in getting me safely to the hotel."

Sam rose quickly from his seat and came around the desk. He grabbed a nearby wing chair and dragged it across the floor. In doing so, it made an obnoxious sound that echoed off the walls. Sam grimaced with embarrassment.

Finally, he set the chair in front of the check-in desk. He was always friendly and personable with guests, but Sam rarely moved a chair to the check-in unless the guest was ill or elderly.

Well, the girl was blind. But that didn't mean she was ill, and certainly, she was not elderly.

"Hello, my name is Sam. I moved a chair for you to sit on. It is about two steps to your left. You must be tired from your journey." He didn't know whether to offer his arm or if he should ask her if she needed help.

He watched in fascination as she took a few steps towards the chair, felt around it, and sat down. "That is very sweet of you. But in truth, the train did most of the work. I just sat and listened to the sounds."

And then she smiled again, and he was now wide awake.

He retook his seat behind the check-in desk and reached for the ledger.

"What name is the reservation made under?" he asked.

"My Auntie's, I believe. Missus Minerva Vaughn. I am Constance Sweet."

Sam's lips twitched with amusement.

Constance Sweet.

It was a darling name.

"Do you find that funny?" she asked.

His cheeks heated at once. He was glad she could not see him blush. "No…I…how?"

"When I lost my sight, other senses strengthened. I don't know how to explain it, but I can tell with certain people when they smile or frown."

"That is amazing."

It was amazing, and especially it interested him as a doctor. "To answer your question though, I think the name is very…"

"Sweet?" She asked, and then she laughed.

She was an absolute doll.

If it were possible to fall in love at once, he had taken the plunge. Well, maybe not love, but a definite infatuation.

"Very sweet," he answered. He paged through the reservation ledger and saw a note attached. He read over it quickly and frowned.

"Is there a problem, Sam?" She asked.

She knew he was frowning. How extraordinary!

"Yes, we received a wire at the hotel from your auntie. Would you like me to read it?"

"Please do."

To Miss Constance Sweet, arriving at The Albion Hotel, December 1, 1892. From Missus Minerva Vaughn. Twin babies afflicted with croup. Will be delayed in arriving. Will send a wire when enroute.

"Oh, the croup. That's terrible," Sam remarked.

He had treated small babies and children afflicted with the croup. While not as bad as diphtheria or whooping cough, it was still a dangerous illness.

"Poor babies," Connie sighed. "They were born so little, and now to be ill again."

"I'm so sorry, Constance," Sam said sincerely.

The coachman pushed open the door, carrying Connie's travel bags as well as a violin case. He placed them near the check-in desk.

"Good night Miss Constance, Sam."

"Good night, Sir," they both said in unison.

"Rather than wake a bellman to carry your bags, I will carry them and show you to your suite, Constance, if that is agreeable to you."

"That would be fine."

He could tell by her depressed demeanor that she was worried for her auntie's little babies. She was also blind, and in a strange town she wasn't familiar with.

"Are you hungry, Constance? I can make up a cold plate from the kitchen and a pot of tea. Unless you wish to go immediately to your suite."

He hoped she would take him up on his offer of a late supper. He was intrigued by this lovely woman.

"I would enjoy a bite of food and conversation. You, Sam, may call me Connie."

"Wonderful, Connie. You just sit there and I will lock the front doors and I will put together two plates of food in the kitchen."

"Thank you," she said with another smile.

Sam walked quickly to the front doors of the hotel and latched them securely. He often locked the doors when he needed to leave the lobby for more than a minute or two. There was no sense in chancing a vagrant entering and finding his way up the stairs to where the guests were lodged, or worse, a thief in the night.

There was a bell outside and above the doors that could be rung if a guest needed to check in and the doors were locked. So there was no worry about a guest being stranded on the outside. Especially now that winter had set in.

Sam walked back to where Connie was sitting.

"The doors are locked. I'm going to the kitchen now."

"Okay, thank you. I'll be fine and still here when you return." He smiled.

There was something about Connie.

It was a joy that radiated from her.

Sam walked into the kitchen and proceeded to turn on the lighting. The kitchen had the best lighting in the hotel. The young lady who was in charge of the kitchen, Miss Lily Rydell, insisted on the brightest lighting. She did not want any of her staff to be burned or cut during food preparation and service.

Lily always joked that the guests would not appreciate blood or burnt skin in their meals. But Sam knew that Lily was of course concerned about the guests, but she was more concerned about the safety of her kitchen workers.

Sam turned on the gas fire of the hob and struck a match and lit the fire. He filled a small pot with enough water for a few cups of tea and set it on the fire to boil.

He often made tea for himself at night, and about twenty minutes before his shift ended, he would put a large pot of water on the hob in the early morning, and prepare a huge urn of fresh hot tea for the morning staff when they arrived for the morning shift.

He wanted to be sure, especially in the winter, that the staff could have a hot drink as soon as they arrived for work.

With the pot of water heating, he went into the larder to see what was left over from the hotel restaurant's dinner service. He was pleased to see a plate of sliced roast beef. Another plate held cubes of smoked ham. There were also nibbles of different cheeses.

He removed all the plates and placed them on a table.

He then checked the dry larder.

There was crusty bread and several leftover ramekins of butter.

He placed the bread and butter on the table next to the meats. He then scampered back to the larder and removed two large portions of chocolate cake with white buttercream layers.

Something sweet for Miss Constance Sweet.

He chuckled to himself at his little joke.

The water for the tea began to boil and he transferred the boiling water into a small teapot that held about four generous cups of tea. He added the tea to the pot and closed the lid to allow it to steep for a few minutes while he set up plates, cutlery, and the food at the table in the kitchen where the staff ate their meals.

When everything was in place, he went back into the hotel lobby, which was just outside the kitchen entrance. Connie was still sitting in the chair, the same as when he had left her. Though she had removed her hat and coat.

"Connie, would you like to come into the kitchen? Everything is ready for you."

"Oh yes, thank you."

She stood up very gracefully.

"Would you like to take my arm and I'll guide you to the kitchen? It's only a few steps away."

"Yes, please."

He held out his arm and instinctively she took his arm with hers and he slowly led her to the kitchen, and showed her to the table and chair, telling her where she was at each step and where the chair and table were.

She reached the chair and felt it all around, and then sat.

"It's all a bit strange when I'm somewhere I'm unfamiliar with," she explained. "I usually have my cane with me, but since the coachman was so lovely about helping me from the coach and into the hotel, I tucked the cane away in one of my travel bags. I had expected my auntie to be waiting for me, and that she would see me to our suite."

"Not a problem, Connie. I will make sure you get safely to your suite."

"I would appreciate that," she said sincerely.

It occurred to him at that moment how vulnerable Connie was.

She had to rely on strangers to get her safely to where she needed to be.

He vowed at that moment that he would become her guide until her auntie arrived at the hotel. When he couldn't be her guide, while he worked, he would spend some of his tip money from the bar to hire one of the younger ladies who worked here at The Albion to be Connie's companion.

He had a few young ladies in mind. Connie might enjoy a companion during her stay until her auntie finally arrived. She would have someone who would be able to lead her around safely, and they could shop and take meals together.

"Okay, Connie," he began. He took her hand and guided her

to a plate. He had set everything up in a square formation for her to find each thing easily. He didn't want to offend her by just going and preparing a plate for her. She wasn't a child, and he was certain she was very adept at living life as a blind person. "This plate is slices of roast beef." He then moved her hand to the next plate. "Cubes of smoked ham." To the next plate. "Orange cheese chunks, thick crusty bread, and a ramekin of soft butter. There is also chocolate cake with white buttercream icing." He then guided her hand to the cutlery.

"I will pour the tea," he said.

"Oh, please allow me to pour the tea," she requested.

"Yes, of course, Connie. If I'm overstepping, please tell me. It won't hurt my feelings. It's only that I've never…" The words stalled in his throat.

He nearly said *I've never known anyone who was blind.*

Not that it was rude, he didn't think, but still, he wasn't sure what the proper etiquette in helping a blind stranger actually was.

"I'm not as helpless as you might believe," she said.

She said it with a smile, so he was relatively sure he hadn't offended her.

Offending her was the last thing he wanted.

"Take a seat, Sam, and I will pour the tea."

He sat down on the hard chair and watched as her slender hands sought out the teapot first.

When she knew where it was on the table, and where the spout was, she then felt around for the tea cups and lined them up on the table. She then placed her finger on the inside of the top of the first cup, right at the place where the cup would be full. Carefully, she lifted the teapot and poured the hot liquid into the cup until the tea touched her finger. She then lifted the pot and moved to the second cup.

She succeeded in pouring two perfect cups of tea without even spilling a drop.

"That's marvelous!" Sam remarked.

He noticed something else as well.

Her eyes tracked.

She hadn't been born blind. Her eyes still were used to moving along with her motions even though they didn't function any longer.

"I attended a very good school for the blind. I was fortunate that my parents were able to provide me with that education. So many blind children end up on the streets."

She frowned and shook her head sadly.

And her sadness made him sad.

She spoke the truth.

Many times he would see little starving children begging on the street corners and most people just passing by them, seemingly looking straight through their pain.

"It is the unfortunate truth, Connie. I wish I could save them all," he said truthfully.

"As do I, Sam. It's the reason I am here. Well, one of the reasons. I was meant to do my Christmas shopping and spend time with my auntie. The other reason is that I have accepted a teaching position at the blind asylum. I will be teaching music, and hopefully a few other subjects as well."

Connie would be living locally at the blind asylum.

Even though he had only just met her, his heart leaped with a certain joy. He wanted to get to know her better.

He hoped that she would want to get to know him better, too.

Yet in his next thought, he wondered why she would want to know him. That thought depressed him a bit. He decided to shake it off and continue speaking before Connie wondered why he was so quiet.

"I admire that so much, Connie. There is occasionally talk around the street that the blind asylum is so very short-staffed – both teachers and physicians. I suppose that the wages are very meager."

"Unfortunately so. The local politicians don't feel that the blind are worth investing in," she said with a deep sigh.

"The blind asylum is so unimportant to the city that it doesn't even have a proper name. It's just referred to as the *blind asylum*.

I am teaching because I am needed and I am wanted. Being blind myself, I am in a unique position to understand the needs of those who are also blind. I would hope the physicians and nurses are there to alleviate suffering, not because they are interested in money or position. Is hotel work your calling?" she asked.

Her sightless eyes were on his face, just as if she was looking at him in an interested manner.

"I work here at The Albion during the day as a barman. I work some nights at the front desk to earn extra money. I have recently sat the medical examinations. If all goes to plan and I pass the exams, I will be a doctor very soon," he said proudly.

He was proud of himself. But he was careful to never boast.

He worked so long and so hard to get into medical school and fund his education. All the long hours of work and study were about to pay off with a medical degree.

At least he hoped so.

"That's quite an achievement, Sam. I wish you luck with your exam results."

"Thank you. I've been told that the results will be posted right before Christmas, usually Christmas Eve."

"It will be an extra happy Christmas for you," she smiled.

He took a sip of his tea and she did the same.

It felt like an extra special Christmas meeting Connie.

He had never been so quickly smitten with a woman. But then again, he had never met anyone like Connie who just shone with light and joy.

He wanted to ask her about losing her sight, but it seemed forward for him to ask something so personal from a woman he only met less than an hour before.

Still.

He was a doctor.

Well, *almost* a doctor.

"Would you mind terribly if I asked you a question about your blindness?"

"Please do. I have no deep dark secrets."

He chuckled then.

"That is good to know, Connie. But in all seriousness, I notice that your eyes still track. I am guessing as a near medical professional that perhaps you were not born blind."

"That is a good guess, Sam. I lost my sight gradually over the period of several years. One fortunate thing about my condition is that I can still make out shapes, and light and dark."

So she wasn't completely blind.

She was almost blind.

But not completely blind.

There were small miracles in this world.

"What is it like?" He asked.

He genuinely did want to know everything about her acquired blindness.

In truth, he wanted to know everything about Miss Connie Sweet.

"How I describe my blindness, what is left of my sight, is when a person who wears spectacles goes into a warm room after they have been outside in the cold winter air, and their spectacles fog, or even walking in the night fog that is so thick you can't make out very much of what is a few feet in front of you. Does that make sense to you, Sam?"

"Yes, very much so."

"But understand, Sam, that I do not harbor any illusions that my sight will stay as it is. I may one day wake up and be completely blind. It is a situation I have been prepared for."

"Let's hope that doesn't happen," Sam said daring to reach across the table and quickly touch the top of her hand.

"Yes, let us hope for that. In the meantime, let us enjoy this lovely food we have before us."

Chapter 2

What a day it had been for Connie Sweet!

It started with her train being late in arriving. Her parents had waited with her at the departure station and saw her safely aboard the train. But because the train had been late departing, it also meant that it was so late that it didn't pull into her final destination station until after midnight.

Thankfully, she had people help her.

A friendly married pair fetched her travel bags and violin case. They then hailed a coach for her and the coachman was also very helpful. He went out of his way to escort her and her baggage into The Albion Hotel, where she was to meet Auntie Minerva.

They had plans to shop for Christmas gifts on the wonderful Carlyle Street that she had heard so much about. They also planned to attend the opera, and perhaps the theatre as well.

That was because Auntie Minerva had visited this town and Carlyle Street a few years earlier for the same purpose

– Christmas shopping. She even stayed at the same hotel – The Albion.

But that wasn't all.

Auntie Minerva had met her future husband on that visit. Minerva said that Carlyle Street was a magical place.

Only to have her return visit delayed, maybe even canceled because her twin babies had croup.

But it was all fine.

Connie was confident in her abilities to navigate even strange cities. The bit of sight she retained meant she could stay out of the way of coaches or avoid being trampled by horses. When others saw her cane, they mostly gave her a wide berth so they didn't bump into her, and she didn't accidentally bump into them.

Yet, there still were thieves and vagrants about who could cause her harm. Her cane made it apparent that she was without sight. They assumed, wrongly, that she was completely blind. The small amount of sight she did retain was a blessing for sure.

Perhaps she would stay a few days at The Albion.

She could have her meals brought to her suite, so there would be no need to leave the hotel.

If Auntie Minerva was to cancel her visit altogether, Connie would contact the blind asylum, her new employer, and inform them that she had arrived early and wanted to start work immediately. Single women were housed in a boarding house of sorts, on the grounds of the blind asylum.

Married couples and physicians were housed in individual cottages on the grounds.

Connie guessed the accommodations were meant as an enticement to work at the asylum for lower wages.

But for Connie, it was the perfect solution to her current

dilemma. She would stay at the blind asylum over Christmas. Certainly, there would be many children who would through no fault of their own, would not be returning to their family homes to celebrate the holidays.

So Connie would celebrate with them.

Life, it seemed always had a way to work things out.

Of course, her blindness had not been a positive thing at first, but luckily she had lost her vision over time, which helped tremendously with the adjustment.

The education she received at the school for the blind enabled her to adjust to life as a blind woman living in a seeing world.

Now, she would share her knowledge and her experience with others who were blind.

She finished the last of her tea, and pat her lips demurely with the linen napkin.

"I believe that I am ready to go to my suite now, Sam. I'm suddenly quite tired from my journey."

She liked Sam.

One of the advantages she found that came with blindness was the ability to sense intent through a person's voice.

Their inflection.

A person can smile and that smile may fool a person into thinking that their intentions were good, even when their intentions were bad. At her blind school, she was taught to always question a person's intentions at first until they gave her a reason to trust them.

With voice, Connie could tell if the speaker was using his or her natural, God-given voice, or if it was strained in some way.

A tip-off that the person's motives might not be so altruistic.

But Sam's voice was lovely and strong...and kind.

Very kind.

And authentic.

As soon as she stood from the table, Sam was at her side, his hand gently at her elbow, ready to guide her to her hotel suite.

"We will leave the kitchen, cross the lobby, and then walk up the two flights of stairs to the second floor, where your suite is," Sam explained. "Once I've shown you around the suite, I will come back to the lobby and fetch your travel bags and violin case."

"Thank you, Sam," she said sincerely.

"It's my pleasure, Connie."

His hand remained lightly on her elbow and gently guided her from the kitchen, across the vast lobby of the hotel, and he counted each step on the staircase out loud to her.

They continued down a long hallway.

"There are rooms on either side of the hall," he explained as they walked. At the end of the hallway, he stopped. "We are now at your suite, Connie."

"A suite for Connie Sweet," she said and then giggled softly at her little joke, not wanting to wake up any of the guests from their slumber.

Sam chuckled along with her.

Yes, she did like this man!

She heard the rustling of keys, and a key entering the lock, turning, and the door opening with a creak.

Sam took his time and showed her all the amenities of the suite.

The carpet under her feet felt thick and luxurious.

There was a lovely featherbed with a satin comforter. She couldn't wait to rest her bones on the bed.

A desk and a chair.

A dresser with several drawers.

A closet to hang her dresses.

But she would do that in the morning when she wasn't so tired.

He showed her with his hand upon hers where the key to the suite lay.

"There is a water pitcher and drinking glasses." He said as he guided her hands from the pitcher to the glasses. "There is a plate here with a few sugar biscuits wrapped in a napkin in case you get hungry before breakfast."

"Oh, that is so lovely," she commented.

Connie made mental notes in her brain about the location of each thing in the suite as Sam pointed it out to her.

"Now, over here, Connie is the…er…ah…" he stuttered.

"Water closet?" she asked.

"Yes," he said.

The relief was apparent in his voice that he didn't need to say the words *water closet*. As if the words were somehow vulgar.

"What is nice about this suite is you have your own bathtub, basin, and…"

He paused again.

"Water closet."

Connie tried to keep her voice even, though she was amused by his shyness. Somehow though, she felt his shyness at using certain words was because he was in her presence. That if she had been a part of a married couple, or a matronly woman, he wouldn't think twice about vocalizing the words *water closet*.

"What color is the suite, Sam?"

She was trying to give him something safer to speak about.

"Oh, it's sort of a muted blue with shades of grey."

"Wonderful," she said.

"I will go and fetch your bags now, Connie."

"Thank you, Sam."

"I won't be long," he said.

She heard his steps moving quickly away from the suite.

While she waited, she sat on the bed. A few minutes later, she heard Sam's steps coming from the hall and heading in the direction of her suite.

"Where would you like your bags and your violin, Connie?" He asked.

"The violin can be tucked in the closet. The travel bags can be placed on the bed, please. I will just need to find my nightclothes. Everything else I can see to in the morning."

She felt the bags being placed on the bed beside her.

"Do you need any help locating anything in your bags?" He asked.

"No, I packed them myself. I know where everything is. But thank you, Sam."

"I have the room service menu for breakfast. Shall I read it to you, and then I can take it to the kitchen for the morning."

"That would be wonderful. I suppose I'm going to be spending all my time here in my suite until my auntie arrives."

She chose the cinnamon French toast, sliced in-season fruit, and tea for breakfast. It was the hotel's most popular breakfast items.

"Connie, I have an idea."

"Yes?" she asked.

"There are several young ladies who work here at The Albion. I am more than certain that one of these fine young ladies could assist you by being your companion. That way you will be able to leave the hotel with them and do your shopping and perhaps enjoy a meal or two together, maybe even go to the theater. You will have some female company."

"You could arrange that?"

"Absolutely," he said.

"I would like that very much, Sam."

"Excellent. I will take care of that in the morning."

Suddenly, Connie was concerned.

"Sam, are you going to get any sleep at all?"

"The front desk girl arrives for duty at 7 AM sharp. I will manage a bit of sleep before my shift in the bar. I have managed this schedule even with my medical school classes. So I am actually getting more sleep now than I have in the last few years."

"I just want to be certain that I am not a burden to you."

"A burden? Connie! You could never be a burden to me. I am more than happy to help you assimilate to not only the hotel but to Carlyle Street and all the surrounding areas as well. There's so much to see and take in." He then paused. "I'm sorry, I didn't mean...see...."

"It's fine, Sam. I suppose I *see* in my own ways. I see in shadows and I see with my hands," she held up her hands, palms out. "I see with my ears, too."

"Of course. I just never known anyone who was blind."

"Now you do."

"Yes, yes I do. And may I say, Miss Connie Sweet, it is my pleasure to make your acquaintance."

She could hear the sincerity in his voice.

Connie had the feeling that Sam couldn't fake sincerity or any other feeling even if he tried.

"And it is my pleasure to make your acquaintance, Mister Sam...no...Doctor Sam..."

"McGreevy." He filled in his surname.

"Doctor Sam McGreevy," she finished.

"Connie…"

"Yes, Sam?"

"I hope you don't consider this as being forward, but would you care to accompany me to dinner tomorrow evening?"

"I would enjoy that very much, Sam. Very much, indeed."

***

Connie woke from a dreamless sleep to a timid tapping at the door.

At once, the evening before rushed back.

There had been the long train ride and the arrival at The Albion Hotel. It was then she was informed that a wire had arrived for her attention telling her that Auntie Minerva was not going to arrive on schedule due to her twin babies being afflicted with croup.

Luck had been with her that she was safely escorted to the hotel by a lovely coachman, and was taken care of by a wonderful young man named Sam, who went above and beyond his duties as the front desk clerk.

"One moment, please," she called out. She reached for the little braille travel clock from the bedside table. She remembered exactly where she placed it before getting into bed for the night.

The clock was a going-away gift from her brother, Charles.

The time was 7:45 in the morning.

Quickly, she felt around at the bottom of her bed for her dressing gown and rose from the bed. Once she was covered by her dressing gown, she carefully made her way to the door of the hotel suite. "Who is there?"

"It is Emma, Miss. I have your breakfast."

Connie felt along for the door for the locks and her fingers worked to open them.

Finally, the door creaked open.

"Good morning, Emma. If you could bring the meal tray into the suite and set it on the table, I would appreciate it very much."

"Of course, Miss."

Emma's voice was the voice of a young woman.

Clear and confident.

Connie could hear the tray being placed on the table and followed the sound. Once at the table, she felt for the chair and sat.

"Miss, Sam has charged me with the privilege of being your companion…your eyes, so to speak, while you are a guest at The Albion. Does that suit you?"

Sam had found her a companion. He was so diligent in his duties.

"I would like that very much, Emma. If it is not a bother to you or if it should interfere with your duties here at the hotel. And please, call me Connie. I am certain we will become very good friends."

"I would like that, Connie. Don't worry about my duties here at The Albion. Miss Lily Rydall, who runs the kitchen, was more than willing to allow me to assist a guest. I think she feels a bit of relief. I'm not a very good kitchen girl."

"Why do you say that, Emma?"

Connie lifted the cloche, and at once the sweet aroma of cinnamon and sugar rose into the air. At once, her stomach grumbled with hunger.

"Let me help you, Miss…Connie."

With her limited eyesight, Connie watched the shadow of

the girl as she prepared her tea.

"I burn the toast and the bacon. I can't cook an egg perfectly to save my life. I also drop things on the floor quite often. Miss Lily can be very salty sometimes, but she puts up with me because she knows I need the job. She says that after the holidays she will arrange for me to move to the front desk."

"That sounds nice. I'm sure you'll meet a lot of interesting people checking in and out of the hotel."

"Yes, possibly. We will see."

"Have you had breakfast, Emma?"

"Yes, all my meals are included as part of my employment. I live at the hotel as well."

"Would you like to have a cup of tea with me? I seem to see another cup on the tray."

"I thought you were blind, Connie! I'm so sorry for my mistake."

Connie could hear the embarrassment and horror in her voice.

"Oh, I am blind, Emma. For the most part. I can see light and shapes. Sometimes even a little bit of color. As I explained to Sam, it is like looking through a very thick fog, or through spectacles that fog over when a person enters a warm room from outside in the cold winter air."

"Ah, I understand now. I would assume this is very positive. Much better than being totally blind." She paused, and then added with her voice dipped low, "I hope I am not saying anything offensive."

"I am not offended, Emma. I prefer that people know my condition and my limitations with my sight. Now, take a seat and have a cup of tea with me and tell me all about yourself."

Emma's figure moved to the available chair across from

Connie and sat.

"There's not much to tell about myself. I am a very boring person."

"Nonsense, Emma! I am sure you lead a very interesting life."

"Well, the hotel has its share of oddities that I find fascinating. At present, I really only deal with staff in the kitchen. Miss Lily doesn't allow me to serve the guests because she is afraid I will drop a tray of food on a guest and then there will be all sorts of trouble. I am very surprised she allowed me to bring your breakfast tray to you."

"I don't think you're as clumsy as you believe, Emma. Perhaps you're not suited for kitchen work. There's nothing shameful about that."

"Yes, I suppose. Anyway, I live here at The Albion. My family lives about a three hours train drive away."

Their situations weren't much different.

Emma left home and traveled a long distance for work.

Connie was doing the same.

"I have also traveled several hours on a train to get here to assume a teaching position at the blind asylum. I will be living on the grounds of the asylum."

"A teacher! That sounds so much more interesting than a kitchen girl or a front desk girl at a hotel," Emma mused.

"Perhaps if you are looking for a change, I could recommend you for a position at the blind asylum. Maybe as a sighted aide. But I warn you that the wages are meager."

"They can't be more meager than the wage I currently earn."

"Do have a long think about it. If you decide you would like a change, I am sure I could arrange a little tour of the asylum."

Connie was speaking the words, but she knew full well that she herself didn't know much about the blind asylum. She was hired by post for the teaching position. She had never actually been on the grounds of the asylum or anywhere near this town.

Lifting the knife with her right hand, and the fork in her left hand, she focused her limited vision on the plate in front of her. The square shape she could somewhat make out was the cinnamon French toast. The shape as well as the smell assured her of that. Carefully, she sunk the knife into the soft yielding bread and cut it into a few bite-sized pieces.

"Would you like me to unpack your travel bags, Connie? While you eat, I can attend to your clothing before it gets too wrinkly."

"Oh yes, Emma. I would appreciate that very much. When I arrived late last night, I was too weary to do more than find a night dress to put on and I fell asleep almost immediately."

Emma rose from the chair and went about moving the travel bags onto the bed as Connie ate her breakfast. The cinnamon French toast was divine. She only had cinnamon French toast which was better tasting during a trip abroad with Auntie Minerva.

Before Auntie Minerva married.

And before Connie had lost her sight.

Connie paused eating as she thought about that last trip abroad. It had only been the summer three years ago, but it was when her sight was worsening by the day. She spent every day of that time trying to memorize every detail of everything around her.

The seaside and the color of the sand beneath her feet.

How the water moved in the crystalline sea.

The smiles on people's faces.

Especially the smiles and laughter of the children.

Every color she saw.

Every shape she saw.

Everything was recorded to her memory.

"Are you okay, Connie?"

Emma's voice broke through her daydream of memories.

"Oh yes, Emma. I was just remembering my last visit to the seaside."

"Well, there is no sea anywhere near here, but Carlyle Street has plenty of pleasant activities to keep you happy before you assume your teaching position at the blind asylum. When you finish your breakfast and dress for the day, I will take you on your first walk around Carlyle Street."

Connie smiled.

"That sounds like a wonderful plan, Emma."

And it really did sound wonderful.

It was going to be a lovely day, Connie was sure, followed perhaps by an even lovelier evening with Sam.

Chapter 3

S am was nervous.

In his small, shabby room on the fourth floor of The Albion Hotel, he inspected himself in the huge cracked mirror that was mounted to the old wooden dresser that held most of his possessions.

The dresser was so old and so overused by so many guests at the hotel in the course of many years, perhaps decades, that if he wasn't careful when opening a drawer, the knob would fall off into his hand. Any day now, he expected the old dresser to crash to the floor in a heap of rubble, fit for nothing more than kindling wood.

Because the state of the furniture did not meeting up with the décor of The Albion, it was moved from a guest room to the staff quarters.

That all happened long before Sam was hired as a barman and assigned the room.

But he didn't mind.

The job had been a God send to him.

His family home had been heaving with relatives all down on their luck. His mother just couldn't say no to anyone who needed a place to stay. There was always shouting, and children and a menagerie of animals running around knocking everything over and eating all the food.

If he had stayed, there was no way he would have ever been able to attend medical college. Living and working at The Albion provided enough wages and tips to live fairly comfortably. He sent a bit of money home each week to his parents and squirreled away the remainder in the bank after paying his weekly college fees.

He would hold on to a small amount of pocket money for sweets or the occasional necessaries he needed.

He couldn't afford to spend frivolously like the majority of his college classmates. Most had access to unlimited funds courtesy of well-to-do fathers or grandfathers. They would all congregate at the local pubs and drink away the evenings and then somehow manage to drag themselves into classes the next morning.

At first, they invited Sam along, but after a while, they stopped asking when Sam always had a reason to say no.

And that was fine.

So quite naturally, Sam also didn't have opportunities to spend any time in the company of any lovely young women. He only had knowledge from his upbringing and the watching of other men on how to treat a lady.

Sure, there were the girls who worked at the hotel. They were always looking for a good time. Their eyes were on the single men who were staying at The Albion on business.

There were also some women who Sam served at the bar.

The women were only slightly above the reputations of the

women who were on display at night in the basement of the hotel.

Sam didn't go anywhere near the no-so-clandestine speakeasy in the basement. It was well-known what went on there every night. The drinking and debauchery. The police were paid to look the other way from the establishment.

But right now, none of that mattered as Sam dragged a comb through his hair which was light in color, but not blond. His eyes were grey, not blue. He was slim, but he wasn't skinny.

He was distinctly average he decided.

What he lacked in social status and looks, he made up for in brains. He was very, very intelligent.

Though he never would say that out loud.

It was his intelligence that earned him a subsidy from the medical college that covered most of his tuition fees. Without the subsidy, he never would have been able to attend medical college.

He brushed away some stray hairs from his suit. Oh, how he wished he could have purchased a new suit for such an occasion as this evening!

His evening with Connie Sweet.

Maybe by this time next year, he would own a closet full of new suits all hand tailored to his measurements.

That is if he not only successfully passed the final medical examinations but also was able to secure employment as a doctor.

Most of his fellow students already had employment waiting for them once they passed the exams and received their licenses to practice medicine.

Several students were sons or grandsons of doctors. They would simply walk into a thriving medical practice.

Others had secured the promise of employment at various hospitals through connections with teachers or other medical professionals.

But Sam was on his own.

His first inclination was to approach the owner of The Albion Hotel, Mister Anderton.

Not only did Mister Anderton have connections to people in all different walks of life and professions, his long-time friend and confidante, Missus Larsen, was the wife of Doctor Anton Larsen, the town coroner.

Sam knew Missus Larsen when she was Miss Rosey Rydall, the former front desk check-in girl at The Albion. She had since married Doctor Larsen and left her position at The Albion. But she was still very good friends with Mister Anderton. She was also the sister of Miss Lily Rydall, the woman who oversaw the kitchen at The Albion.

It was through Miss Lily, that Sam, for a very token sum of money, was able to secure a companion for Connie while she was in residence at The Hotel, or until her auntie arrived. Miss Lily was sympathetic to Connie's predicament of being both nearly blind and alone in a strange town, and offered the services of one of her kitchen girls, Emma.

Some even sensed that Miss Lily was a bit relieved to have Emma spend time away from the kitchen. In truth, everyone knew that Emma was hopeless as a kitchen girl. Miss Lily, though a formidable boss in the kitchen, had a soft heart that she rarely showed anyone. Rather than dismiss Emma from her employment, Miss Lily was having Emma trained to work as a front desk check-in girl.

So, with the close connections that Mister Anderton shared with Missus Larsen, her husband Doctor Larsen, and Missus

Larsen's sister Miss Lily, perhaps Mister Anderton could put in a word to Doctor Larsen about considering Sam for a position in the coroner's office.

Asking Mister Anderton for such an enormous favor, was not something Sam relished the thought of. Still, a reference from Mister Anderton would go a long way in securing gainful employment.

Not that Sam really wanted to start his career as a doctor working with the dead.

Yet with no familial connections or waiting employment, he didn't have many options available to him.

A few months or perhaps a year or so working diligently at the coroner's office would hopefully put him in good stand for a recommendation for a job in a hospital treating living patients.

But right now wasn't the time to dwell on his future.

It was time to go to the hotel lobby and meet Connie for dinner.

***

Sam entered the lobby from the back staircase of the hotel.

The lobby was bustling with guests coming and going from the hotel. As busy as it was at that moment, it would get even busier as the Christmas holiday was fast approaching.

Soon, the lobby would be transformed into a Christmas wonderland of sorts. An enormous pine tree would be sourced, chopped down, and transported to the hotel lobby.

Tinsel and garland would be hung on the walls, the front desk, and just about anywhere it could be attached. Several fresh pine wreaths would also be acquired and hung throughout the lobby, with the largest wreath being placed on the front door of the hotel.

Miss Lily also saw to all the holiday decorations, and like her kitchen, she expected nothing but the best.

Currently, some guests in the lobby were checking in, but most were on their way out for dinner followed by the theatre or some other form of entertainment. Others were in town on business matters and headed to the hotel restaurant, followed by a stop at the hotel bar. A few regular and trusted guests would exit the hotel, walk to the back, and enter the basement for more lively entertainment at the speakeasy.

These trusted guests were few and far between though.

Most were long-time patrons of The Albion and its amenities.

In truth, the vast majority of guests at The Albion had no idea of the thriving business in the basement. Or those who knew of it had dismissed it as a rumor.

Sam moved through the throng of guests, his eyes looking left and right for the lovely Connie Sweet.

Finally, he saw her, and he stopped cold in his tracks.

Dressed in a deep blue frock, her hair up in some type of fancy knot, Connie sat demurely upon one of the plush velvet hotel chairs. Her coat over her lap, and her hands folded on top of her coat. Her fur hat and gloves were on a nearby table.

She simply…shone.

Connie Sweet was a sweet breath of beauty and sunshine.

At that moment, Sam was sure he was falling in love with this beauty, even though he knew so little about her, and that any feeling he thought he felt was really for naught as Connie was embarking on a career of her own as a teacher at the blind asylum.

Still, there was a tiny hope within Sam that Connie would want to keep in touch with him. After all, she would still be living close enough to visit frequently, if that was something she wanted.

Then the doubt he so frequently felt crept over him once more.

That feeling of inadequacy he so often felt among his fellow students at the medical college.

That he didn't belong there among them, and that they too, knew he didn't belong. That he was not of their social circles.

Why would Connie want to remain in touch with him on a social basis?

It was true that she hadn't spoken much of her family or background, but she was intelligent and well-educated. Her manners and dress were that of a privileged young woman.

And he was only hoping to pass his medical exams with the hope of possibly obtaining an entry-level position at the coroner's office on a favor from his employer.

A man trying to control three small children as they ran around his legs accidentally bumped into Sam and jostled him out of his deep thoughts.

It was only then he realized he had been staring at Connie.

He hoped beyond all hope that no one noticed.

It would be the end of his future if he was branded a lecher.

He straightened up, rolled his shoulders and inhaled a deep breath of courage, and strode directly to where Connie sat.

"Hello Connie, it's Sam."

At once, her face broke into a jovial smile and she let out a merry laugh.

"Yes, I know who you are Sam."

His cheeks heated.

Thankfully she couldn't see it.

He was already mortified. Red cheeks would only add to his embarrassment.

"Yes, of course, you know who I am. I'm sorry. There are just so many people in the lobby that I wasn't sure if you could recognize my voice among so many others."

He hoped his excuse was acceptable. He decided to opt for a change in the subject matter.

"Connie, are you ready to leave the hotel? We have reservations at The Carlington. It is a nice eatery with fine food."

"That sounds lovely."

As she began to stand, he gently took her arm and guided her to her feet. Taking the fine velvet coat that matched the blue of her dress, he helped her into her coat.

"Thank you, Sam."

Her skin was alabaster with a hint of pink in her cheeks and lips. Hair pins studded with ivory pearls were precisely placed into her hair which was the color of fallen oak leaves dusted with golden shimmer.

He then handed her hat which she carefully placed on her head, followed by putting on her gloves. Finally, Sam placed her blue beaded reticule in her hand.

He wanted to tell her how pretty she looked.

Beautiful, in fact.

But he was afraid of overstepping.

So he said nothing.

"Let us go now, Connie."

Chapter 4

⚜

Connie held Sam's arm as he led her from the cold wintery Carlyle Street into the warm restaurant.

Right away they were attended to by a pleasant hostess who took their coats and hats and showed them to a table.

At once, Connie recognized the aroma of fresh seafood.

Perhaps lobster or maybe boiled turbot.

It was a pleasant smell, not rancid or greasy.

The sign of a good eating establishment.

"Sam, could you please describe the restaurant."

It had become quite natural for Connie to ask whoever accompanied her on her travels away from her home to describe her surroundings. As it was right now, all she could make out visually was large shapes of furniture and people walking about.

"Well, Connie, it is a nice setting. It is a very large dining room and almost every table is occupied. There are many tables scattered throughout the room. Some tables are for a sitting of two diners, some tables are larger, and set for four or more diners. The tables are dressed in red cloth and the napkins are white cloth. There is a very large saloon-type bar in the adjoining room. It's not shabby at all. A string quartet is in one corner of this room setting up their instruments to entertain the guests."

"And the menu?" she asked.

There was a pause. Connie assumed that Sam was doing a quick read of what food was on offer.

"There is a starter of olives stuffed with anchovies. A soup choice of macaroni or hare. The fish selection is boiled turbot in a lobster sauce or fried eel. The entrees are a choice of mutton cutlet in tomato sauce, roast gosling, and partridge or duck. If you prefer, they have a sweet omelet or deviled sardines on toast, or cheese, bread, and salad." He summarized the menu.

Connie was pleased that her sense of smell was on point. She had accurately recognized the aroma of turbot and lobster.

Since her blindness, she had become well adept at eating without spilling or spotting her clothing. Still, she was cautious in public, and this evening, she would be even more cautious while dining with Sam.

That meant she needed to choose her food carefully.

"I believe that I will have the cheese, bread, and salad plate, please."

"Are you sure you don't want something more substantial, Connie?"

She placed a hand over her heart.

"Oh, Sam, I had a very large lunch at the Tessley Tearoom with Emma. The cheese, bread, and salad plate will suit my appetite this evening."

It wasn't a lie.

She did have a very large delicious lunch with Emma at the

Tessley Tearoom. And if she got peckish later on, she had a selection of teacakes and confectionaries waiting back in her suite at The Albion that she purchased while out and about on Carlyle Street with Emma.

"What will you be having this evening, Sam?"

"I am going to start with the anchovies stuffed olives followed by the boiled turbot."

The figure of a woman appeared next to their table. Connie knew from the woman's shape it was a different woman than the hostess. There were a few soft thudding sounds followed by the rush of water.

Connie deduced that the water glasses had been set on the table and filled.

"Are you ready to order?"

The woman's voice was young sounding and sweet. She probably wasn't much older or younger than Connie herself, she guessed.

"The lady will have the cheese, bread, and salad," Sam said in a clear, firm voice. "I will have the anchovy stuffed olives, followed by the boiled turbot."

"Very good, Sir and Miss."

There was a lull in the conversation when the waitress parted ways from the table. Connie was taught to be a lady and not to continuously dominate the conversation with a gentleman. But she sensed Sam's nervous disposition. Perhaps he, too, was afraid of coming across as overbearing or dominating.

It was quite sweet, actually.

She didn't know Sam well – yet. But she knew he was a fine young man.

Just as she was about to ask about his medical studies, the waitress returned to the table. This time Connie recognized the shape she placed on the table.

It was a wine bottle.

Two crystal wine goblets were then set down and the woman began to pour wine from the bottle into the glasses. At once, the fruity but tart smell of wine entered Connie's senses.

"We didn't order wine," Sam said, almost sheepishly.

"Compliments of Mister Thaddeus Anderton and his companion, Miss Rydall."

Connie recognized the names of the owner of The Albion Hotel, and that of the hotel's kitchen supervisor who helped Sam arrange for Emma to become her companion for the duration of her stay at The Albion, or until Auntie Minerva's twin babies were well enough for her to travel and leave them behind with their father and grandparents.

In her limited vision, Connie watched as Sam stood and lifted his glass, turned his body and motioned to someone, presumably Mister Anderton and his guest, and made a wide gesture of thanks.

He then retook his seat.

"How lovely of your employer and his companion to send over wine," Connie said.

"Yes, Mister Anderton is a very generous man. I am quite indebted to him for his kindness and flexibility that allowed me to live and work at The Albion while attending medical college."

"Mister Anderton surely recognizes what a fine, upstanding man you are, Sam."

"Oh…I ah…" he sputtered. "Connie, tell me about your day. What did you do, where did you go?"

Connie was thrown momentarily by the abrupt change of subject. Clearly, Sam wasn't comfortable with being praised.

Connie liked that.

Sam could have easily been boastful or ungrateful for what he had been given, but he was humble and sweet.

"Well, Sam, Emma and I did a bit of shopping on Carlyle Street. I didn't purchase any Christmas gifts yet because Emma has informed me that the shops will be acquiring and displaying their Christmas stock in the next few days. So it would be prudent to wait until then to shop for gifts. I did purchase some teacakes and confections from that lovely little shop run by the older woman."

"Miss Elenora Grass." Sam filled in the name. He knew the names of most of the shop owners on Carlyle Street.

"Yes. That is her name. We then went to the very large department store where I purchased a pair of warm gloves for Emma because her hands felt very cold to me when she was leading me around Carlyle Street. She did not want to accept the gloves, but I insisted she have them as a thank-you for taking me on during my stay. I had the distinct feeling that she had no gloves of her own."

Just saying the words made Connie feel a bit sad.

She had grown up with all the things a girl, then a young woman needed, and more. When her health declined, the finest doctors were procured by her father. When the diagnosis of impending blindness was uttered, instead of tears and fretting, her parents sought out the best school for the blind for her.

Money was never an issue.

Now she could spend some of her own money treating others but hoping to not offend them with her gifts. She wanted to purchase something nice for Sam as well. His kindness could not be overlooked. Yet the perfect gift had not shown itself to Connie in her mind just yet.

"That was very kind of you, Connie. I don't know Emma very well, but I know she traveled far from home seeking employment. Much like you, I suppose."

"Yes, Emma and I talked about our similarities in leaving home and traveling many hours on the train to begin a new phase of our lives. Emma has even mentioned the possibility of joining me at the blind asylum as a teaching aide."

"Is that possible?" he asked.

"I believe so. From my understanding, the blind asylum is woefully understaffed. No one wants to work with the blind, or for low wages. So the asylum offers what enticements it can to gain staff. Unmarried women are housed on the grounds in a sort of boarding house setting. Married couples and physicians are housed in separate cottages on the grounds of the asylum without cost to any member of staff, be them physician, nurse, teacher, housekeeper, or whatever their job may be."

"I did not know this, Connie. I don't think many people in town know this either. Perhaps if it was well known, the asylum might attract more qualified staff."

"I think that from time to time they do take out advertisement space in the local newspaper. But maybe it is buried so deep into the back of the newspaper no one reads it. Or maybe the blind asylum has a terrible reputation for wages that no one believes things can actually get better."

"But you believe, Connie."

"Yes, I do believe, Sam."

She did believe that things would improve at the blind asylum for both staff and more importantly, the students. But in truth, she didn't know. All she ever heard was how poorly staffed they were. How the students' education was below average. She wouldn't truly know the state of her new employment until she arrived there formally on the second of January, or if Auntie Minerva could not travel, she would check in before Christmas and settle in among the students.

A few minutes later, two shadowy figures appeared next to the table.

Sam stood at once.

"Mister Anderton, Miss Lily, I would like to introduce you to Miss Connie Sweet. She will be assuming a position as a music teacher at the blind asylum after Christmas."

"It is lovely to meet you both," Connie said with an endearing smile. "Thank you so much for sending over the wine. It is delicious."

"We won't interrupt your dinner, Lily and I just wanted to introduce ourselves."

"I'm so pleased that you have. I hope to meet you again very soon."

"I'm sure we will," Lily said and she gently touched the top of Connie's hand.

"Thank you both for being so kind," Sam said sincerely.

"Our pleasure. Have a wonderful evening," Thaddeus Anderton said.

Connie waited until the couple moved away before she spoke.

"They seem like a very nice couple. Very generous," Connie remarked.

"Yes, they are."

"Are they married?" Connie asked.

"No, their relationship is…a bit unclear to me."

"How so?"

"I can only guess that Miss Lily is Mister Anderton's companion. They spend a lot of time together."

It wasn't unheard of in this day and age for a couple not to be

43

married but to spend significant time with each other. However a couple felt comfortable and happy, that was all that mattered.

"Well, good for them. I don't know them, but for some reason, I sense they are very happy," Connie said.

"Yes, I believe they are happy," Sam agreed.

After they finished dinner, they walked slowly up Carlyle Street to The Albion.

"I had a lovely evening, Sam," Connie said.

"I did as well, Connie. Thank you for spending time with me."

She laughed then.

"You don't have to thank me for spending time with you. I enjoy being with you. Very much so."

"So, you would consider spending even more time with me?" He asked.

She could hear the uncertainty in his voice. He was nervous. It made him even more endearing to her.

"Yes, Sam, I would love to spend more time with you."

"Wonderful. Wonderful, Connie."

As they continued to walk, Sam had a bit more spring in his step, she noticed.

He was happy.

She was happy.

Ever since arriving at Carlyle Street and The Albion, when things first looked so bleak with Auntie Minerva needing at home to tend to her sick twin babies, everything turned around so beautifully.

She met Sam.

Because of Sam she met Emma and had a new friend.

Could life get even better she wondered as they entered the hotel?

Sam walked her upstairs and into her suite.

"I'll stop in the kitchen and ask them to send up a pitcher of fresh water and a small pot of tea," he said. "Is there anything else I can get you or do for you before I say goodnight?"

"No, you've done so much already. Thank you for dinner, Sam."

"You're very welcome. Well…I guess I should be going now."

"Good night, Sam. Sleep well."

"Connie?"

"Yes?"

"Could I kiss you good night?" he asked.

A zing of happiness zipped through her.

"Yes, I would like that. Very much so."

His lips descended to meet hers.

Closed mouth.

Soft.

Sweet.

Perfect.

"Good night, Connie Sweet. Sweet Dreams."

The smile was still on her lips when he closed the door behind him.

And the smile remained on her lips until she closed her eyes that night to sleep.

Chapter 5

⁌

S am couldn't sleep.

The kiss he shared with Connie was more than enough to keep him awake and happy.

But the wonderful evening and the sweet kiss were overshadowed by a note left under the door in his room that he found when he returned after saying goodnight to Connie.

The note was from Doctor Peter Scopes, the lead instructor at the medical college.

It instructed Sam to appear at the office of Doctor Scopes at 8 AM sharp the next morning.

The results of the final examinations.

But Sam was sure he heard through other students that the results weren't to be released until Christmas Eve.

So what did this sudden summoning to the college mean?

Had he failed his final exams?

It had to be.

Suddenly, Sam felt unwell.

Very unwell, indeed.

For once in his life, things had been looking up.

He had been blessed with a medical school education. It was something he never took for granted. He studied hard. He was certain he had performed well in the final exams.

Maybe his overconfidence became his curse.

How would he face his family and tell them he failed?

His coworkers at the hotel would soon find out.

And Connie.

He had just become acquainted with the most beautiful, intelligent woman who seemed to like him as well.

He couldn't face her again if he failed.

But that would be the coward's way out if he disappeared.

No, he was a man, and he strove to be an upstanding man.

He would tell Connie the truth, no matter what the outcome.

After a sleepless night of spinning scenarios in his head, he finally dressed and made his way out of the hotel, and hailed a coach.

When he arrived at the office of Doctor Scopes, he wasn't present, but many of his fellow students were. There was a certain excitement in the air.

On the closed door of Doctor Scope's office was a sheet of paper tacked to the door.

Sam weaved through the other students who were excitedly jabbering on to each other. Sam was too concerned with what was written on that paper to hear what was being discussed around him.

As he got closer, he saw it was a list of names.

Even closer, and he read the words:

Final examination results.
  Successful students.

If your name is on this list, you are invited by Doctor Peter Scopes to his home for a celebration. You may bring a guest.

The time, date, and place of the event were listed.

Sam went down the list of names that were in alphabetical order. Finally, he reached the M's.

There was only one surname beginning with the letter M.

Doctor Samuel McGreevy.

He had done it.

He passed the exams.

He was now a doctor.

All the worry was for naught.

It was then Sam realized he had been holding his breath and inhaled deeply followed by a deeper exhale.

It was then he was besieged by his fellow students – no, his fellow doctors with hearty handshakes and loud congratulations.

He belonged now.

He finally belonged.

He was someone.

He was Doctor Samuel McGreevy.

Life, as he now knew it, had changed forever.

And for the best.

Chapter 6

⌒⟋⟍⟍⟋⌒

C onnie was the first person he needed to share his good
news with.

Sure, he hadn't known her for very long, but she
was now always on his mind.

It had to be love because he never felt this way before – ever.

After a celebratory drink with his fellow new doctors, he had
tea rather than indulging in anything of alcoholic nature so
early in the day, he accepted a carriage ride from Joseph Adler,
who had also received his results that morning, back to Carlyle
Street.

He bid Joseph goodbye and a thank you, and hurried into the
hotel, taking the back staircase two steps at a time and made
his way to Connie's suite and knocked at her door.

His heart was beating so fast.

Emma opened the door. Connie was at the table sipping her
coffee.

Connie! I passed my final exams! I'm a doctor! *I'm a doctor*!"
He shouted.

She pat her mouth with the linen napkin and quickly got to her feet and held out her arms to him.

"Sam, I am so very proud of you!"

Whatever love he already felt for this woman doubled at that very moment. He lifted her off the floor and then set her down and danced her around the suite. The happiness he felt was so strong it was palpable.

"Connie, I need to let my parents know, and I need to take care of some business. Will you have enough to do to occupy yourself today?"

"Yes, Emma and I will be heading out to shop on Carlyle Street again. You do what you need to do."

Her hand went to his cheek.

"Again Sam, I am so very proud of you. Congratulations on your accomplishment."

"Thank you, Connie."

"Congratulations, Sam," Emma chimed in.

"Thank you, Emma."

"I will see you later on, Connie."

"I will be waiting," she said.

And he knew in his heart that she would be waiting for him.
***

Sam gathered his courage and rapped a few times on the door jamb of Mister Anderton's open office door.

"Enter!" Mister Anderton called out.

He couldn't run now or change his mind.

It was too late.

He had to see through what he wanted to ask for from his employer. Even if Mister Anderton took offense to his request and fired him from his employment on the spot, it didn't really matter. He could return home and reside temporarily with his family. His savings would hopefully see him through until he secured employment in some capacity as a doctor.

Mister Anderton looked up from the paperwork in front of him on his expansive oak desk.

"Hello, Sam."

"Hello Sir," Sam said awkwardly.

"Don't just stand there in the doorway. Come inside my office so we don't have to shout."

Sam guessed that Thaddeus Anderton was around forty years old. He had hair that was almost black in color, olive skin, and hooded eyes.

He always dressed impeccably.

His hair and beard were always perfect.

No one knew much about his upbringing or whether he was an educated man.

Thaddeus Anderton was brilliant.

He was a powerful man.

Probably the most powerful man on Carlyle Street who owned all but one hotel in the town.

From Sam's understanding, Thaddeus Anderton could be a man's best friend or his worst nightmare. But he had always been kind and benevolent to Sam, as well as the other staff of The Albion.

Sam forced himself to walk confidently into the office and then stopped near the chairs that sat empty in front of the desk.

He certainly would not sit down uninvited.

This wasn't a social visit.

"Take a seat, Sam," Mister Anderton commanded.

Sam sat.

Before Sam could state his purpose for this uninvited visit to his employer's office, Mister Anderton spoke.

"Sam, I've been meaning to ask you, have you received the results of your exams yet?"

This surprised Sam a bit.

He didn't think for a second that Mister Anderton remembered any details about his daytime barman and occasional nighttime front desk check-in person. But it made him happy that he had made at least a small bit of an impression on Mister Anderton for him to remember that he had sat the medical exams.

"Yes, Sir. I have passed all my exams. I am now a doctor."

It felt so surreal to say those words, *I am now a doctor.*

At once, Mister Anderton jumped to his feet and came around his desk to which Sam got to his feet as well.

"Congratulations, Sam! Congratulations!"

Mister Anderton gripped Sam's hand and shook it firmly.

"Good job, Sam. I'm proud of you."

And with Mister Anderton saying those words, Sam felt his very own sense of pride.

His employer, the King of Carlyle Street, was proud of him.

"Is there something you need, Sam?"

Mister Anderton didn't return to his seat. He stayed standing. Suddenly those feelings of inadequacy crept back into Sam's body and snaked up his spine.

"Well, Sir, the lead instructor from the medical college, Doctor Peter Scopes, is hosting a party at his home this Saturday evening to celebrate with those students who have successfully passed their exams. A sort of celebration mixed with a Christmas party."

"Oh, I know Scopes. He's smart, but he's also a bit of a pompous ass," Mister Anderton commented.

It was true.

Scopes was a pompous ass, but he was more than just smart. He was also successful and admired by those in and out of the medical profession.

No doubt about it.

"I was wondering, Sir, if you might possibly have an old suit of clothing that I might borrow for the occasion since we are about the same size." He felt his face flush. "You see, the young lady I have been keeping company with, Connie, has agreed to accompany me to Doctor Scopes' party. I know she cannot see, but I still would like to look presentable, if at all possible. For the entire time that I attended classes at the medical college, I have worn the same two sack suits that I have alternated wearing. I'm sure that it has been noticed by both my fellow students and the lecturers."

The office room fell silent except for the ticking of the mantle clock.

It was Mister Anderton who broke the silence.

"Sam, grab your coat. We're going out."

***

"Oh, Mister Anderton, I can't accept this. You are far too generous. I would be so grateful to borrow a suit of old clothing from you that you no longer wear."

Sam stood in the middle of the floor inside *Jackson's Clothing for the Discerning Gentleman.* The clothing shop catered to men of status and wealth.

Just like Mister Anderton.

Two tailors were measuring Sam.

One measuring his leg, and the other measuring his back and shoulders for a jacket. Sam tried with all his might to keep his legs from shaking.

"It's Thaddeus, Sam. No more Mister Anderton."

"Thaddeus, I can't…" He whispered, knowing the two tailors who were taking his measurements for a new suit were listening to every word.

"Sam, you don't become a doctor every day of the week. It's a momentous occasion that we must celebrate. You are going to walk into Doctor Scopes' home with your lovely lady friend on your arm, and you will be looking every inch the young doctor. Just accept this is happening."

Sam knew with certainty he couldn't stop it if he wanted to.

He vowed at that moment in time that someday, hopefully, sooner rather than later, he would be able to somehow, someway show his appreciation to Mister Anderton…Thaddeus… for all he had done for him in the past, and for all he was doing for him now.

"Thank you so much. I will make you proud," Sam said solemnly.

"I'm already proud of you, Sam. Just remember in the future, if you can help someone who is trying their mightiest to succeed, then do so. Money is fluid. If you have it to give, you give it. If you need money, you take it when it is offered. It's that simple."

That he would most certainly do. "I promise."

"Oh, and add a coat as well. Black," Thaddeus ordered.

When the measurements were completed, and the fabrics were chosen, Sam stood in a bit of a daze at the counter of the fine men's clothing shop while Thaddeus Anderton instructed the tailors on what to provide and when to deliver it to The Albion.

"Mister McGreevy, your suits will be delivered to The Albion. The deliveries may be a bit staggered. But most certainly, your attire for your upcoming function will be with you in plenty of time," the clerk informed him.

"Actually, it's Doctor McGreevy," Thaddeus corrected the clerk.

"Oh, pardon me. Doctor McGreevy. We look forward to serving your clothing needs now and in the future."

"Thank you so very much," Sam said sincerely.

"Okay, Sam, let's go," Thaddeus said.

Sam assumed they were returning to The Albion.

But, Thaddeus walked briskly down Carlyle Street in the direction away from the hotel. Sam could do no more than keep stride with the older man.

Thaddeus stopped abruptly in front of a shop that traded in leather goods and luggage. Once inside, the intoxicating smell of expensive, premium-quality leather filled Sam's nostrils. He had never been inside this particular shop before.

He had never a need to visit this shop.

Apparently, until today.

Perhaps Thaddeus was planning on traveling over the Christmas holiday. Maybe visiting family.

"I had been thinking recently about your sitting the medical exams, and what type of gift would be most appropriate for you when you successfully completed and passed your exams."

He stopped and gave Sam a smile.

"It was actually Lily who made the excellent suggestion that a doctor's bag would be appropriate." Thaddeus lifted a dark brow. "Do you have a bag?"

Heat crept up the back of Sam's neck.

After treating him to what amounted to a new wardrobe of the finest men's clothing and footwear not just on Carlyle Street, but anywhere near and far that well-dressed affluent men frequented, was Thaddeus actually going to purchase Sam his first doctor's bag?

"No, Sir…" he paused and corrected himself. "No, Thaddeus. I was planning to purchase a cloth bag from one of the street sellers."

"Rubbish!" Thaddeus thundered. He then snapped his fingers to catch the attention of the old clerk who was leaning up against the counter having what looked to be a spirited chin wag with an equally old woman.

"Mister Anderton!" The old man immediately walked away from the old woman.

She did not look pleased by the interruption.

"Did you receive the doctor's bag I ordered? For my friend, Doctor McGreevy," Thaddeus placed his hands on Sam's shoulders, "Has successfully passed his medical exams and the doctor's bag is in order."

"Yes, yes, I have Doctor McGreevy's bag in the back. It's all engraved to your specifications and ready to take away."

Sam stood quietly, absorbing the realization that Thaddeus Anderton had already been planning to present him with a gift for his officially becoming a doctor.

Sam was deeply touched.

He knew Thaddeus Anderton was a good man.

A man who treated his employees well and fairly.

But this…

To actually remember that Sam was finishing his medical school education, sitting the exams, and had faith that Sam would successfully pass his exams. Well, this was a lot to digest.

The old man made his way through a curtain and disappeared into the back of the store. While he was gone, Sam watched as Thaddeus had a browse through the shop. He decided he should browse as well, rather than looking like a wooden statue.

His legs freed up and his eyes took in all the quality travel cases. There were some expensive tapestry travel bags for ladies. On a wall next to the window was a selection of buttery soft kidskin gloves for ladies.

Would Connie like something like that for Christmas?

His eyes then set upon a case full of beaded silk reticule bags in all colors from the palest white to the jeweled blues and greens. The bags reminded him of the little blue beaded bag that Connie carried with her on their first dinner out together.

Beside the reticule bags were framed ladies' bags with leather handles.

He would definitely visit the bank this week and withdraw some money and return to this shop to purchase a bag for Connie as a Christmas gift.

"Sam?" Thaddeus called.

Sam walked quickly to where Thaddeus stood holding two ermine-trimmed leather ladies' handbags. Sam had seen some of the more affluent women both at The Albion and on Carlyle Street carrying these larger bags.

"Yes, Thaddeus?"

It was so strange calling Mister Anderton by his first name!

Thaddeus held the bags up in front of him.

"Do you think Lily would like one of these bags…or both?"

He was actually him for his opinion now!

Sam surveyed each bag.

One was dark brown in color.

The other a shade of ivory.

"Well, I think Miss Lily would very much like one of these new-style bags. They are very modern. It is only my opinion, but the darker bag seems more suited to an older woman. I believe the ivory shade would suit Miss Lily better. Plus, I notice that Miss Lily seldom wears any color except white."

Thaddeus tilted his head in consideration and then nodded his agreement.

"I believe you are correct, Sam. I'm glad you came along. I needed a younger man's opinion."

"I am happy to help."

"Yes, this one!"

Thaddeus exclaimed and placed the darker bag back on the display stand just as the old man came back through the curtain and into the showroom of the shop.

The old man carried a dark-colored bag with gold closures. He sat it on the glass counter and began rubbing it down with a cloth.

"Is this to your liking?"

Sam wasn't sure if the old man was asking him or asking Thaddeus.

Thaddeus stepped forward and lifted the bag into his hands and clinically inspected every inch of the leather surface, and every corner. He then set the bag on the counter and tested the closure a few times by opening and closing it.

He then checked the gold plate.

Sam's heart sped in his chest when he saw the name engraved in an elegant script on the gold plate:

Doctor Samuel McGreevey.

Thaddeus then handed the bag to Sam.

"What do you think, Sam?"

The bag might as well have been a piece of fine art sculpture. His hands trembled ever so slightly.

"I think it is the most beautiful bag I've ever seen, Thaddeus."

Thaddeus' lips broke into a smile of satisfaction.

I don't know how to thank you, Thaddeus. I feel like…I feel like I'm still dreaming of this day. That any time now I'm going to wake up in my bed at the hotel."

Thaddeus burst out laughing and slapped Sam good-naturedly on the back.

The old man came out from behind the counter and took the bag from Sam. "Would you like the bag delivered, Doctor McGreevy?" His accent was heavy and thick.

"Please, Sir. Could it be delivered to The Albion?"

"Uh huh, uh huh," the man mumbled and scrawled his name, Doctor Samuel McGreevy, in the care of The Albion Hotel on a piece of paper.

"And I will need this added to my account, wrapped securely, and delivered to my office," Thaddeus said and handed over the ermine handbag.

Miss Lily was a lucky woman, Sam thought. Thaddeus treated her like a queen.

Sam hoped that he, too, would soon be in a situation to treat Connie like a queen, too. For the very first time ever, Sam felt enough of a man to marry a woman as beautiful, smart, and of course as sweet as Connie Sweet.

Yes, he only knew Connie for a short time. But in that time he had fallen in love with her.

Life continued to get sweeter all the time.

Chapter 7

It was finally time for Sam to begin cultivating his social status.

The carriage, not rented but borrowed from Thaddeus Anderton, slowly crept up the street of palatial homes in the neighborhood of Doctor Peter Scopes, physician, surgeon, lecturer, philanthropist, and childless widower.

Scopes, who was about the same approximate age of Thaddeus, came from money as did his father before him. Apparently gained from the import business. Tea, spices, coffee, and other things as well.

Some legal, some not so legal.

None of that mattered now.

Sam held Connie's slender hand which was covered by a cream-colored kidskin glove. She wore a gown of a rich jeweled green color. Sam had no knowledge of cloth or what was silk, tulle, gauze, velvet, or anything else.

Except for lace.

He knew what lace looked like. Her warm wrap matched the

gown perfectly.

Her hair was swept up into a crown of curls, and emerald studded pins accentuated the style.

Whatever the fabric, Connie sweet looked as perfect as a portrait painted by one of the old masters and hung in a gallery for all to admire.

He had already presented her with a wrist corsage of white roses adorned with a festive bow.

He wore a black superfine dress coat, a pair of well-fitting trousers also in black, and a black vest. The waistcoat was low to disclose the shirt front with small gold decorative studs and black tie, not cravat – Thaddeus insisted that cravats were on their way out of fashion – and a white linen cambric handkerchief. On his feet were a pair of patent leather low-heeled boots. He also wore an overcoat, hat and gloves, in line with the cold winter evening weather.

He never felt happier in his lifetime.

He was in love!

He wanted to shout it from the rooftops.

He was in love and he was a doctor.

It still boggled his mind.

"Do you think there will be dancing?" Connie asked.

There was excitement in her darling voice.

"I am sure there will be."

As the carriage crawled to a stop, Sam reached into his pocket for the small box.

He was nervous.

It was his first real gift to Connie and he hoped she would like it.

"Connie, I have a little something special for you."

He placed the small square white box into her hands.

"For me? What is the occasion?"

"It is just a little something to let you know how I feel about you, Connie."

She removed her gloves. Her fingers lifted the small lid and felt for the gold bracelet with its small green and clear stones.

"Oh, Sam! It is simply magnificent! I can tell just by touch. Could you please describe it to me?"

His heart thudded like a lovelorn schoolboy who dared to get close to the object of his affection. He gently removed the bracelet from her hand.

"It is a golden color with lacy links and stones of green like your lovely dress, and clear stones that sparkle like the stars," he described as he fastened it to her delicate wrist.

"I do believe that the bracelet is beautiful, but not as beautiful as you, Miss Connie Sweet." He dared to press a kiss against her palm.

Her palm then traveled to his cheek and rested there.

"Thank you so much for the beautiful gift, Sam. I shall treasure it always."

"Connie?" He was pleased his voice spoke her name clear and strong, not in a shaky squeak.

"Yes, Sam?" Her hand remained on his cheek.

"I know that we have not been acquainted for very long, but I must speak my mind."

"Of course."

"I love you, Connie Sweet. I think I have loved you since the moment you walked into The Albion that first night. I love everything about you."

"Even my eyes?" Her voice had a touch of laughter.

"I love your beautiful brown eyes, Connie. I love you."

It felt so liberating to Sam to voice his feelings out loud to

62

Connie.

"I love you, too, Sam McGreevy. Doctor Sam McCreevy."

She kissed him then and his life was almost complete.

***

Connie felt like she was being carried away on a cloud high above everything and everyone but Sam.

He loved her!

She loved him!

Although she never spoke her feelings out loud, even to her most trusted confidante, Auntie Minerva, since her blindness overtook her, she feared she would never find true love.

At the school for the blind, they were gentle, but firm, when telling pupils that their blind condition would make the search for love complicated. Men of status and wealth preferred a sighted woman, even one who was of questionable reputation over a sightless woman, even a woman whose sight wasn't completely absent, like Connie.

She had been cautioned to tread carefully when men approached her in an overly familiar way. That the man's true intentions should always be vetted by a trusted man in her life such as her father, uncle, or medical or legal professional.

Well, it was almost the year 1893, and Connie Sweet needed no man to vet Sam McGreevy. She was in charge of her life and made her own choices.

Sam helped her from the carriage, and she took his arm and they slowly strolled up the winding pathway to the grand home of Doctor Peter Scopes. She was always cautious and a bit nervous as well whenever she visited any new surroundings.

Tonight was no different.

Hopefully, she would adapt quickly. Even with a large number of people about.

63

In her very limited cloudy grey window of sight, she could tell the house was the largest on the street. Sam was careful to enlighten her with every step and every little turn they took. They stopped at the open door and a voice welcomed them inside.

The floor of the entrance hall had the feel beneath her feet of fine marble. The first scent she encountered was that of delicate flowers and the smokiness of an open fire somewhere in the home.

"Doctor McGreevy, welcome, and thank you for attending our little celebration this evening."

The voice was strong, older, and distinctly male.

"Thank you so much for the invitation, Doctor Scopes. Let me introduce my companion, Miss Constance Sweet."

"So lovely to meet you, Miss Sweet."

"Please, call me Connie. No need for formalities," she said with a smile she hoped was pleasant.

"Connie," he corrected himself.

"Connie is new in town. She has accepted a position as a music teacher at the blind asylum," Sam added.

"Marvelous!" Peter exclaimed. "We must talk later if that is suitable for you. I have questions."

This was an interesting turn of events," she thought to herself. "Of course, Doctor Scopes."

"Peter," he corrected. "I look forward to it. In the meantime, I hope you both have a wonderful evening, and I look forward to speaking with you both as time permits. For now, come in, eat, drink, and let us all be merry."

Sam led her through the long entrance hall and stopped to whisper, "He is brilliant, but is also quite pompous as well."

"Just promise me that you'll never become pompous," she

whispered back.

"Cross my heart and hope to die if I ever turn pompous."

She couldn't help but laugh as quietly as she could so as not to attract attention.

"We're at the ladies' dressing room, Connie. There are maids here to take your wrap and assist you with anything you might need."

Before she could say a word, she was whisked away by a maid who removed her wrap and then straightened her gown, followed by repositioning a few arrant hairpins. Connie was a bit disoriented. She was in a home she wasn't familiar with, with people she didn't know who were all around her in constant motion, and she hadn't brought along her cane.

She only hoped the maid attending to her knew that she was blind.

"There, beautiful," the woman said in a heavily accented voice.

"Can you please take me to my companion? I am not able to see."

"Oh, yes, Miss. Let us try to find him."

As Connie was led from the dressing room, she realized the maid most likely didn't know who Sam was. It felt like she was being led in circles, and soon she was becoming disoriented.

One of her biggest fears. She silently cursed her blindness.

"Connie, is everything okay?"

The voice belonged to Peter Scopes.

"Oh Peter, no, I seem to have lost Sam. I believe he went to the gentleman's cloakroom to check his coat and hat."

"May I take your arm?" he asked.

"Yes, of course. Please do."

As soon as he firmly took hold of her arm, Connie relaxed. She was safe now.

"There must be a very long line at the cloakroom, or perhaps Sam has got lost in conversation with some of his fellow students, or should I say, fellow doctors."

"Yes, perhaps so."

"Well, he hasn't gone far. Let us get you something to eat before the dancing begins."

Peter led her to the refreshment room. Connie didn't mind. In fact, she found herself a touch irritated by Sam's disappearance. He knew her limitations, especially when she was in public in a strange environment.

"Connie, there is substantial food, fowl, ham, tongue. Do you like cucumber?"

She really wasn't in the mood for any type of heavy food or meat. Perhaps a bit of cake she could enjoy.

"I do like cucumber. I find it quite interesting, Peter. It all sounds lovely, but I am really in the mood for something sweeter."

"Of course. I had the town's finest confectioner and baker bring in the sweets. There are iced buns, biscuits, trifles, cakes, and even tipsy cakes. Would you like coffee or tea?"

"I believe I will have an iced bun and coffee, please, Peter."

She could just make out his shadowy figure in her limited vision as he prepared a plate for her with an iced bun, and then he fetched her coffee, presumably from an urn on the great table. He then returned to her.

"I'm sorry, Connie, I should have seen you to a comfortable chair with a table before I prepared your refreshment."

He took her arm and guided her through the throng of people.

"That is quite alright, Peter. Unless you are experienced with the blind, you don't think about it," she said as she settled onto a comfortable velvet wing chair.

He departed but returned quickly, and described in detail, the bun, the coffee, the cutlery, the plate, the napkin, and the china cup the hot coffee was in, and even the table.

She appreciated his help, especially since her escort, Sam, seemed to have vanished, at least for the present. Peter was probably correct that Sam got lost in a moment of excitement with a few of his former classmates, now doctors as he was.

Connie was surprised when Peter took a seat across from her.

"Connie…perhaps now isn't the time to ask…"

She could hear the hesitation in his voice.

"By all means, Peter, speak your mind," she said as she nibbled the corner of the iced bun.

"My niece, her name is Sophie. This past year has been unkind to her. She was suddenly struck blind."

Connie felt the weight of unpleasant emotion fall over her.

"I am so very sorry, Peter. I am certain your family, especially your dear niece, is devastated."

"Yes, it has been quite a blow from above…for all concerned."

"Was it an illness?" She ventured a guess.

"She did experience a bout of scarlet fever in the past. But, she seemingly recovered. The blindness took us all by surprise."

"I can understand. With me, it was a different onset. My vision slowly deteriorated to the point it is now."

"I notice your eyes track, so I knew you weren't born blind, and that you could relate to poor dear Sophie."

"In a way, yes, but it is so very much worse for your niece. She had no time to prepare for the inevitable as I did. Is she attending a good school for the blind?"

She asked the question, but, like herself, Sophie came from a fine family. Surely she was receiving a stellar education and instruction on adapting to her blindness.

"I am afraid not, Connie." He paused before adding, "She refuses to leave her room most days. She just sits alone or stays in her bed with the door closed. She must be coaxed to do anything, even to eat or bathe."

Connie nodded.

She understood far too well.

"So, how can I help, Peter? Would you like me to recommend the school I attended? Somehow I don't think you would want your niece attending our local blind asylum."

It was sad but true.

When she accepted the teaching position at the blind asylum, she knew what she was getting herself into, and that was a woefully understaffed asylum with students who came from poor families who could not pay for their education, or even more unfortunate, the families who cast out their child because they became too troublesome and useless with their blindness. They abandoned them at the blind asylum and never looked back.

That was the main reason Connie accepted the teaching position.

These poor unfortunate children needed as much love, attention, and help as she could provide to give the children a chance at a life outside the asylum walls.

"Yes, Connie, I would very much appreciate a recommendation. And…" he hesitated.

"What is it, Peter?"

"Would you consider visiting my niece and just speaking to her? I am hopeful that if she meets with you and can understand that there still is a full life to be led, just like with you, then perhaps she will be more amenable to attending a school."

"Yes, absolutely, Peter. I would be happy to meet Sophie and share my experience. Do know though, that it may take Sophie a long time before she is able to accept her condition and allow herself to be trained to live life as a blind woman."

"I do understand that, Connie. Anything you can do to help is very much appreciated. We are all at the end of our ropes now with Sophie. No one can get through to her."

"Sophie's denial is not uncommon, Peter. There were many young women at my school who refused at first to leave their rooms. They were frightened of the unknown and frightened for their future. They knew that their lives would never be the same. The students who were born blind are the most fortunate, in my opinion." She stopped speaking to place a hand on her chest. "Because they never knew sight, so they grew from infancy to adulthood always adapting to the world around them.

Sophie's blindness is the cruelest of them all. To suddenly just lose her sight. It will take much time and patience from both Sophie and her family for her to accept her condition and learn to thrive as a blind woman, as I have. But it can be done, Peter. I promise."

"Well, there you are."

She heard Sam's voice next to her chair. He had finally returned. She saw Peter's shadow rise from his chair.

"Thank you for introducing me to this lovely young woman, Sam. She is a delight." Peter then said, "Connie, I'm looking forward to a dance with you this evening, and I would love to set up a meeting between you and my niece, at your convenience, of course."

"Yes, Peter. I certainly would enjoy a dance, and we will set up a time and day for me to meet your beloved Sophie."

69

Connie watched through her limited foggy vision as Peter exited and Sam took a seat beside her.

"I'm sorry I got held up at the coat check. Peter hired a photographer to photograph all the new doctors separately and together. It felt like it took forever."

"Not a problem, Sam. Peter was here to walk me to a seat and to fetch me an iced bun and coffee. We had a very nice talk."

"It seemed quite personal," Sam said.

"Yes, it is a personal matter, but I'm sure Peter wouldn't mind me telling you. His niece, her name is Sophie, has recently lost her sight."

"Oh, that's tragic," Sam interjected.

She could hear the concern in Sam's voice in just a few words. It made her love him even more.

"Yes, especially since there was no warning. Peter and his family are very concerned for Sophie. She refuses to attend a school to help her adapt to life as a blind woman. She is even refusing to leave her room. Peter has asked me to visit Sophie, and of course, I said that I would."

Sam took her hand into his.

"You are an amazing, inspiring woman, Connie Sweet. I love you more with each passing moment."

He pressed a kiss against her palm and her heartbeat raced.

"And I love you, Doctor Sam McGreevy, more with each passing moment."

And with those words, the music began.

Sam stood.

"Miss Connie Sweet, would you do the honor of dancing with me?"

She held out her hand to him and he guided her to her feet.

"Yes, Sam, I would love to dance with you."

Chapter 7

And so they danced, and danced...and danced.

Chapter 8

❦

After a fairy tale night in which Miss Constance Sweet felt every bit a princess after spending her evening with her prince, Doctor Sam McGreevy.

She lay in her bed in her suite at The Albion Hotel, fingering the stones on the bracelet he had presented her earlier in the evening. Now that the night was over, she could linger in the memories of it all.

When she woke in the morning, it was to a knock at the door.

She had grown accustomed to Emma's knock.

Today they were going somewhere special.

To the blind asylum.

Sam was accompanying them.

The visit was for Connie to meet with the staff and get a feel for the environment before she moved into her room. Her other possessions would be arriving by train and post after the new year. A wire had been sent to The Albion and delivered and read to Connie by Miss Lily. Though the twins had recovered, Auntie Minerva could not leave them. She sent her regrets.

But that was fine. The recovery of the twins was what was most important.

Connie had already met the love of her life, Sam, and she had also made a wonderful friend in Emma. She was even secretly hoping that Emma would be offered and would accept a position at the blind asylum, perhaps as a sighted teacher's aide. It would be lovely to have Emma around her all day.

She was a bit nervous about living away from home, where she was comfortable, and moving into the blind asylum and working a job as a teacher.

But accepting the teaching position was a step towards independence. The last thing Connie wanted was to be dependent on her family for the remainder of her life.

"Come in, Emma!" She called.

Connie heard the key turn in the door, the lock snap open, and the door creak open. After being at the hotel for the past few weeks, it was a sound she had grown accustomed to each morning when Emma arrived with breakfast.

"Good morning, Connie. I brought a light breakfast of fresh bread, butter, jam, and marmalade, as well as coffee. Since we're traveling to the blind asylum, I didn't think you would want anything heavy in your stomach."

Emma was so sweet.

She was always considering what Connie needed.

"Good morning, and thank you, Emma. Bread and jam sound a delight."

Through her misty vision, she watched Emma's figure place the tray on the table, and begin to pour the coffee.

"Emma, are you wearing a brown dress by any chance?"

Emma immediately stopped what she was doing and rushed to Connie.

"Yes, yes I am wearing a brown dress today! Can you see me?"

There was such excitement, true happiness in her voice at the thought that Connie could suddenly see again. It endeared her to Connie even more.

"Very occasionally, I can distinguish colors. Today is one of those days, but it will not last very long though."

Emma hugged her and pressed a kiss against Connie's cheek.

"Let us hope it lasts long enough for you to see Sam."

She didn't want to tell Emma that the limited bit of color she could see didn't mean she could make out facial features very well. In the fog of vision she did maintain, today was simply a day that a little color penetrated the fog.

"Let us hope so, Emma."

Connie made her way to the table, felt for the chair, and sat. Emma had already laid out her breakfast for her.

The bread was buttered and slathered in cherry jam. The coffee was poured and the cream was added.

"Thank you, Emma."

"My pleasure, Connie. I will get your clothing laid out for today while you eat. Is there a particular dress you wish to wear to the blind asylum?"

"Something a bit festive, I should think. Christmas is only days away. I believe there is a dark red dress in the closet and matching boots."

Connie took a bite of bread and chewed it carefully. After she swallowed, she sipped her coffee. The food was always so tasty at The Albion.

"Any word from your Auntie Minerva?" Emma asked as she went about retrieving the dress from the closet."

"Yes. Miss Lily brought a wire to me yesterday before I went off with Sam to Doctor Scopes' party. She won't be able to make the trip to The Albion. But the good news, the twin babies have fully recovered. So, thanks be to God for that miracle."

"Oh yes! That is good news indeed. I'm sorry your auntie could not travel."

"Yes, it is a bit sad, but there is also a bright side. I met you, Emma. Your friendship means so much to me."

"I feel the same, Connie. As soon as we met I wanted so badly to be your friend."

Connie smiled.

"Then we both got what we wanted. A friend for life."

***

Sam finished dressing in front of the cracked mirror in his room at The Albion.

He still couldn't believe that he was wearing such a fine suit of clothing. He touched the fabric, and once again felt so incredibly grateful for Thaddeus Anderton's friendship. Even as a new doctor, he couldn't expect to make much money.

Not yet anyway.

He hadn't even secured employment yet.

But on Christmas Eve, he and Connie were invited to Thaddeus' home for a gathering. Doctor Larsen from the coroner's office, who was the husband of Thaddeus' good friend and confidant, Missus Rosey Larson, and the brother-in-law of Miss Lily would be in attendance. Perhaps he could have a word with him about possible employment.

It would be a busy Christmas Eve.

First, he and Connie would visit with his family, and then later, they would be off to Thaddeus' gathering.

He hoped Connie would like his parents. He knew his mother was a bit overbearing at times, and his father a bit coarse. Connie was used to fine manners. But he couldn't dwell on his parents' possible behaviors, or in truth, any of his family and extended family's behaviors. Today was the day to accompany Connie to the blind asylum to meet with those in charge and tour the facility.

He wanted to be looking his very best not only for those at the blind asylum who were sighted but for his Connie as well.

Once he was satisfied with his appearance, he took his coat from the closet and carefully laid it over his arm, and retrieved the two small, festive broaches made of red berries and pine that he had purchased from a child seller on the corner of Carlyle Street.

One broach was for his beloved Connie, the other for Emma. It didn't feel right to him not to treat Emma as well. The girl had been such a help to Connie since her arrival at The Albion, and Connie now considered Emma a cherished friend.

He left his room, locking the door securely behind him, and took the back staircase to the floor where Connie's suite was. He barely knocked at the door when the door flew open, and Emma, wild-eyed and skin flushed, exclaimed, "Hurry, Sam! Connie is seeing color. Hurry and allow her to see you before it goes away."

He rushed into the suite and saw Connie standing in the middle of the entry room.

She was a vision of Christmas loveliness.

Dressed in a dress of deep red, her hair was swept up into a fancy knot, and a matching bow, not too big and not too small, but just the perfect size, was pinned to her beautiful gold-dusted hair.

"Connie! You look beautiful!" He exclaimed.

"Thank you," she said sweetly, and her smile was radiant.

"Is it true? Can you see a bit of color today?"

"A bit, not too much. I can see that Emma is wearing a lovely brown dress. I can see your suit is very dark, perhaps a very dark blue."

"Yes! My suit is blue." In his excitement, the thought that maybe she could see him and make out his features a little more clearly suddenly concerned him.

What if she didn't like how he looked?

"Are you okay, Sam? You're frowning a bit," she said.

"Oh, no, no, I'm so incredibly happy for you to experience this little bit of extra vision."

"Shall we be on our way?" She asked. "I want to spend whatever time I have with this little bit of color in my life looking at all the Christmas decorations."

"Carlyle Street looks very festive," Emma remarked as she helped Connie into her coat.

"I have this little broach for you, Connie. For your coat. And one for you, too, Emma." His voice was almost shy now. After all, it was just two little broaches."

"Oh, thank you, Sam! Can you please pin it to my coat?" Connie asked.

"Yes, of course."

He handed a broach to Emma, and carefully pinned the other broach to Connie's dark-colored coat."

"I can smell the pine. It's lovely," Connie sighed.

"The broach is very cute. It's got little red berries around a sprig of pine," Emma explained.

Sam marveled at how quickly Emma adapted to working with Connie's blindness. Miss Lily had made the right choice of kitchen girls to assign the job as a companion for Connie.

"Well then, ladies, let us venture out into the cold and off to the blind asylum." He took Connie's arm and led her out of the room and Emma locked up behind them.

He was careful to go slowly so that Connie could take in whatever sight she might be able to make out in her limited vision. He pointed out the great Christmas tree in the lobby of the hotel as they passed through, carefully guiding her around the large crowd of people checking in for the holiday.

Once outside, he hailed a coach and helped Emma first into the coach, and then Connie beside her before he gave instructions to the coachman and then settled in beside Connie.

The ride began with a bit of stop-and-go.

There was much traffic on Carlyle Street and the streets surrounding it. Always a busy street, it was even busier due to the impending Christmas holiday. Both locals and visitors alike were browsing for that last-minute gift. House staff members crowded the butcher shop, the spice shop, the greengrocer, and the bakeries getting in everything needed for holiday meals and parties.

The further they got from Carlyle Street the more the crowds thinned out and the roads became a bit rougher and the coachman slowed the pace to keep from having an accident. Finally, they arrived at the massive wrought iron gates of the blind asylum. A great distance from the gates set the enormous building that housed the asylum itself.

The winter skies added an extra element of forlornness to the old building and its surroundings all closed off by the gates.

Yet, Sam felt a modicum of relief that his beloved Connie would be safely behind the gates and inside the building. And then a weird, almost sickly feeling came over him. It was then he realized that Connie would be here at the asylum attending to her duties as a music teacher, and he would be…somewhere.

Practicing medicine.

He hoped.

Nothing was certain.

It was entirely possible that he wouldn't be able to find employment in the area, and might need to travel and set up a living situation elsewhere. If that occurred, it was almost certain that he would lose contact with Connie. Maybe there would be letters exchanged between them at first, but how long would it last?"

The squeak of the coach's door being opened by the coachman jolted him back from his disturbing daydream. At once, Sam guided Connie from the coach, and when she was standing firmly on the ground, he helped Emma from the coach and closed the door.

"Please wait here for us to return as we agreed," Sam told the coachman.

"Very good, Sir. I will be here reading today's newspaper and awaiting your return."

"Thank you."

Emma held onto Connie's arm as Sam pushed open the gates and then waited until both women passed by him and onto the asylum grounds. He then closed the gates behind them and firmly took Connie's arm and the three of them walked slowly toward the large foreboding building.

It was a bit amusing to Sam that Emma described the building to Connie as being like a fairy castle. Sam certainly would not have called it a fairy castle, but it wasn't as horrible and rundown as he had been led to believe by rumors and supposition of the citizens of Carlyle Street.

It was clear that none of them had ever been on the grounds of the asylum.

"To the right of the main building and a bit of a walk it would seem are several cottages," Sam explained. "I assume these are the cottages that you mentioned, Connie, that house the married staff and the doctors."

"I suppose there is no reason to tour the cottages since I am neither married nor a doctor," Connie said.

But *he* was a doctor.

And they *could* be married.

But before he would consider the possibilities any further, a rotund balding gentleman and an older woman emerged from two large wooden doors.

"Miss Sweet! We have been anxiously waiting for your arrival. Come in! Come in!" The jovial man called.

Sam didn't know the man, that was certain, but he liked him immediately.

The trio walked towards the couple.

"Three steps my darling," Sam said as he guided her up the stone steps which were in a good condition.

He found that it was becoming quite natural to both himself and to Emma to describe everything for Connie.

"Hello, you must be Mister Caldwell. I am pleased to meet you," Connie said with a friendly smile. "These are my companions, Miss Emma Jane Lovell, and Doctor Samuel McGreevy."

"Pleased to meet you, too, Miss Sweet. I have with me Missus House. She is the headmistress of the asylum…" he paused and cleared his throat. "Well, we are in the process of moving away from the term *asylum* and onto using the word *academy* to describe our institute."

"I think that is a very wise decision, Mister Caldwell. The world is changing quickly." Connie then shifted to the woman. "It is lovely to meet you, Missus House. I am sure we will get to know each other quite well."

Chapter 9

C onnie was quite impressed with the blind *academy*.
A part of her had fears that the academy would
be some terrible, almost workhouse-type of environment and that the building would reek with the smells of vomit and urine.

But it wasn't anything like that.

Though the halls were a bit chilly, the classrooms were very warm.

And the children!

Connie was delighted to meet the students. They seemed eager and excited to meet her as well. Their reception was so overwhelming that Missus House and two other teachers, Miss Kline, who was partially sighted, and Miss Redford, who was fully sighted, had to gather the children and force them back to their classrooms to continue their studies.

And the children loved Sam and Emma, too!

They continued the tour, being shown the hall where meals were served. Chickens were roasting, Brussel sprouts and carrots simmered on the hob, while large pans of bread stuffing were being removed from the ovens in anticipation of lunch.

"That smells divine!" Emma exclaimed. "As good as the food at The Albion!"

"Well, that is high praise indeed, Miss Lovell," Mister Caldwell said with a hearty laugh.

"Emma has been working as a kitchen girl at The Albion for quite a while, but over the last few weeks, she has been my sighted companion when Sam has had to work," Connie commented casually, hoping to plant the seed in Mister Caldwell's mind that might quickly grow into a job offer for Emma. "Emma so easily adapted to working with me, a blind woman. I believe she would be an amazing sighted teacher's aide, and in no time, a full teacher."

"Is that so, Miss Lovell? We have several openings here at the academy. Perhaps you would consider joining us? Miss Sweet certainly thinks very highly of you."

"And I of her, Mister Caldwell. I would be very interested in working here at the asyl...*academy*, perhaps alongside Connie, if possible. I would love to train as a teacher, as well. It would be a dream for me to teach children."

"Well, what a wonderful day it is! I am sure we can realize that dream for you, Miss Lovell."

The affection Connie felt for Emma doubled.

Emma was now more than just her paid companion and guide.

She was now her friend.

They toured the staff quarters for single women, which were housed in the same building, one floor above the children's floor.

Sam was asked to wait in Mister Caldwell's office along with

Mister Caldwell, as it was a *women's only* floor.

No men permitted.

Missus House led them to the front staircase that led to the women's staff quarters.

The teachers, nurses, and office staff rooms were a generous size and private. Each contained a bed, a bureau, a closet, a desk, a chair, and an adjoining water closet shared between two women.

The other staff rooms, for teacher's aides, housekeeping, kitchen workers, child care attendants, medical aids, and other miscellaneous female staff were much smaller private rooms with a bed, bureau, desk, and chair. The water closet facilities were shared. Missus House also showed them three double rooms that could be shared by two staff members, perhaps sisters, but there was never enough staff to occupy those particular rooms.

"Let us now go back to Mister Caldwell's office and enjoy a cup of tea and perhaps a slice of cake," Missus House said as they finished the touring of the women's quarters. I do hope that the two of you will enjoy your time here at the academy and find the experience rewarding. We need you both very much, and no matter what you may have heard about the academy, we are a very tight-knit little community here."

"I never listen to rumor, Missus House. As soon as I was told about the teaching position, I knew without a doubt it was my calling."

That was the truth.

Even before Connie applied for the position at the blind academy, she had heard the wonderful story from Auntie Minerva about the magic of Carlyle Street.

She had already fallen in love with Carlyle Street.

But it was nothing to the love she felt for Sam.

Yes, it was very quick to fall in love with him. But love wasn't always logical. You had to grab a hold of it when it arrived and hold on tight.

And that is exactly what Connie would do.

***

Sam sipped his tea as he sat alone in Mister Caldwell's office. The older man had been called away to see another visitor but had promised he would return momentarily.

Now, in the quiet and warmth of the office, Sam looked at the oil paintings of the patrons of the academy that hung on the walls. A fire burned in the ornate fireplace.

The blind academy was nothing like he had been led to believe.

It wasn't a lunatic asylum.

People weren't running around the halls in rags, screaming and crying.

The staff looked content and not a bit stressed or overworked.

The food served to the children was appetizing, and the children were clean, adequately dressed, and looked happy enough in their surroundings.

For being sparsely funded by the local government, and relying heavily upon donations from wealthy patrons, the academy, though a bit understaffed, was a lot nicer than anyone on Carlyle Street gave it credit for.

And that had included Sam.

Until now.

Mister Caldwell lumbered back into the room.

Before he could speak, Sam asked, "Would it be convenient for you to show me your medical facilities? And perhaps afterward, when Connie and Emma return, you could give me and Connie, and Emma if she cares to join us, a viewing of the cottages you have set aside for married doctors?"

The rotund man's face broke into a huge grin.

"Are you considering joining us as well, Doctor McGreevy?"

Sam nodded. "This academy needs Connie. I need Connie. I also need a job, and you need a doctor. I feel in my heart and in my bones that I need to be here. If you'll have me."

"And Miss Sweet…you two?"

"I plan to ask Connie to be my wife."

"Well, I think that is marvelous. Love is marvelous, Doctor McGreevy. I also feel in my heart and my old bones that you belong here, too."

Sam stood and shook his hand to close the deal.

"Let us go to the academy's medical facilities. I am anxious to see where I will be working."

***

Sam waited while Mister Caldwell went to find the lead physician of the blind academy, Doctor Jesse Alvin.

Before Mister Caldwell disappeared down the hallway, he introduced other medical staff. There were two capable-looking nurses and a helper.

They all seemed pleasant enough.

The best thing about the medical wing of the building was its clean smell. The medical facility itself was, like the other parts of the building, old. The equipment had seen better days and was in needing of replacement, but would still be serviceable for a few more years perhaps.

It would do.

Besides, Sam thought it was best to not start his career in some modern environment with the newest equipment.

It wouldn't always be like that, that was certain. If he had started out in a modern hospital, when or when he chose to move on, it would be tough going to a facility with older equipment. So the blind academy was a good first choice to launch his career as a doctor.

It was better than the alternative, which was asking for a position at the coroner's office. Though not the worst employment he could imagine. No, the worst was the lunatic asylums and the prison. He had seen both firsthand and would rather languish behind the bar serving drinks at The Albion for the next thirty years or so, then go mad himself attending to lunatics or prisoners.

So, being up to his elbows in entrails every day at the coroner's office was slightly above that. From what Sam heard from others at his medical college, the position at the coroner's office paid well.

And who knew? Doctor Anton Larsen, the head coroner, seemed to not only survive, but thrive in the environment.

But for Sam, it just wasn't where he wanted to be. It was also true that he could be deluding himself into even thinking Doctor Larsen would hire him.

Once again, he would need a favor from Thaddeus Anderton, whose very good friend, Rosey Larsen was the wife of Doctor Anton Larsen. Still, Sam knew he couldn't continually go to Thaddeus for favors. The man had already gone above and beyond for him. Now that Thaddeus saw him as a friend, more or less an equal, he did not want to lose that connection or friendship.

The blind academy was the place he needed to be.

He would be able to support his wife.

If Connie said *yes* to his proposal.

But why would she?

Connie came from a well-to-do family, he came from slightly above abject poverty. His family would be in a much better financial situation if his mother didn't constantly allow her family members, able-bodied adults who refused to work, to live under her roof. His father, who worked hard and long hours in a factory was spineless and acquiesced to her.

Connie could do so much better than him as a spouse.

Her blindness had nothing to do with her attracting wealthy, influential men.

Such as Doctor Peter Scopes.

Sam sensed immediately at Doctor Scopes' grand party that he was deeply interested and fascinated by Connie. Sure, he used the excuse of his blind niece to engage her in conversation and even went as far as inviting her to his sister's home later today to meet his niece.

Of course, Connie would never turn down a person in need, and Doctor Scopes was sure to impress upon Connie how much his niece needed to be counseled.

Finally, the footsteps echoing off the old academy walls and heading in his direction broke up his morbid thoughts.

Thankfully.

Mister Caldwell introduced the academy's lead and until Sam's arrival today, only current physician, Doctor Jesse Alvin.

Doctor Jesse Alvin was an interesting-looking fellow. He was tall and wiry, not much older than himself, Sam guessed, and it was very apparent that Doctor Alvin was missing an eye.

He surely fit in well at the blind academy, Sam thought to himself as he extended his hand to his new employer.

"Jesse Alvin, meet Sam McGreevy. Sam has just received his exam results and happily has passed. He has agreed to join you here in the medical wing." He then once again excused himself from the room.

"It is a pleasure to meet you, Sam," Jesse shook his hand firmly. "I need you here. Our little scamps are always getting themselves into mischief and come here with bumps and bruises. Luckily, we are fairly well insulated so we don't see much influenza or any other nasties."

"Thank you for giving me this opportunity, Doctor Alvin. I am looking forward to moving onto the grounds and beginning work."

"It's Jesse, and believe me, you are most welcome here. I have a feeling we will become very good friends," he smiled.

"I agree," Sam smiled back. He liked Jesse Alvin right away. It was just a feeling that he was a good person, and Sam only wanted to be associated with good people.

"You are probably dying to ask me where my eye disappeared to, so let's get that out of the way," Jesse grinned.

Sam never would have asked the man about his eye ~ well, his lack of an eye. At least not until he knew the man better. But he had to admit to himself that he was curious.

"It's not a glamorous story by any means. It wasn't the war or some act of chivalry or bravery. My brother poked me with a shoemaker's awl when I was six years old. Bye-bye eye, bye-bye sight." Jesse shrugged his thin shoulders. "At least I have sight in one eye. It doesn't make me completely know the feelings or the experiences of the children here at the academy, but I do understand loss and partial blindness. It makes me aware of how important my seeing eye is." He pointed to his good eye.

"Yes, I can understand that. My lady friend, Connie…Miss Connie Sweet, who accepted a position here at the academy as a music teacher, has lost a great deal of her sight. She has told me that she has prepared herself for the day she could lose the limited sight she still retains."

"Well, let us hope that day never happens. For Miss Sweet or myself."

"Amen."

Suddenly, Sam heard Connie's voice in the hallway coming in their direction. She was cooing and talking sweetly to someone with her.

"Here comes my Connie now."

"I will be delighted to meet her." Jesse's face broke into an affable grin. "She also has one of my favorite and frequent little patients with her."

Connie walked into the room with Emma at her side gently guiding her at her elbow. In Connie's arms was the sweetest-looking little girl with mouse brown curls and cheeks splotched from crying.

She couldn't have been more than three years old. Just a babe, really.

Seemingly very young to be a student at the academy.

A babe who appeared to be blind, and should still be at home being nurtured by her doting parents.

Yet here she was.

"Florence, you are back again? What did I tell you about roughhousing with the other children? You are much too young and tiny," Jesse gently chastised.

"Florence was accidentally knocked over by one of the new students who is still finding her way at the academy," Connie explained as she pressed a kiss against the child's cheek.

Sam's heart warmed immediately at the sight of Connie with the child.

"Florence, we have a new doctor joining me soon at the academy. His name is Doctor McGreevy, and he is a friend of Miss Connie."

"Hello, Doctor," the child said, but it sounded to the ear as *Hell-wo, Doctro*.

Jesse then looked at Connie. "It is a pleasure to meet you, Miss Sweet. I am Doctor Alvin, but do call me Jesse. Sam has told me you, too, are joining us at the academy. Welcome."

"Please call me Connie. I'm delighted to meet you as well, Jesse."

"So what is ailing you, Florence?"

She touched her finger to her little bottom lip which was slightly swollen.

"Oh, poor darling!" Jesse exclaimed and had a long look at the child's lip. "Did you bump your head or twist an arm or leg?" he asked.

"No," Florence answered.

"Will a sweetie make it better? Jesse asked.

"Yes! Think it will," Florence perked up immediately at the mention of a sweetie.

Jesse went to a table and retrieved a large mason jar full of sugar sticks. "My ma makes these," he said unscrewing the top of the jar and removing a sugar stick, and passing it to Sam.

"Here is your sweetie, Florence," Sam said placing the sugar stick into the child's little hand.

At once, Florence began licking the sugar.

Suddenly, Missus House appeared.

"Alright Florence, it's time to return to the school room."

At once, Florence clung to Connie. The sugar stick fell from her hand and dropped to the floor, breaking into pieces. "No! Stay with Miss Connie!"

Emma dropped to her knees and gathered the pieces while Jesse took another sugar stick from the jar.

Connie rubbed Florence's back sympathetically.

"I will be seeing you every day very soon, Florence. Right after Christmas, I will be moving into the academy and teaching music."

"Can I go home with you for *Cistmas*?"

Sam watched as Connie's cheeks flushed red with emotion and her eyes swelled with tears.

"I wish I could take you home with me for Christmas. But I am staying at a hotel, Florence. It is not a nice place for a little girl. It is only adults," Connie explained.

"Can you come here for *Cistmas*?" Florence asked.

There was so much hope in little Florence's voice that Sam had to blink a few times to keep his own emotions in check.

Connie's eyes moved to Sam. He wasn't sure at that moment how much her limited vision allowed her to see, and if the colors she had been seeing earlier in the day had gone away. He touched Connie's arm.

"Yes, Florence, I will escort Miss Connie to the academy to spend some time here on Christmas. I promise."

Florence sniffed at the little berry and pine broach on Connie's coat.

Without hesitation, Emma removed her broach, looked to Missus House for permission, and when granted, she attached her broach to Florence's dress.

"Now you have your own little pine broach, Emma said sweetly. "But you must not eat it! It will get you very sick!"

"*Tank you*," Florence said in the sweet little voice that squeezed Sam's heart.

"You are very welcome," Emma said and gently pat the child's head.

"Come along now, Florence. Miss Connie has an appointment she must attend this afternoon."

"I will be back for Christmas, I promise, Florence," Connie whispered to the child and sealed her promise with another kiss on her cheek.

Missus House then took Florence from Connie and Emma handed Florence the sugar stick, and they disappeared down the hall. Missus House's black sensible shoes echoed off the walls of the hallway as she walked, the sound growing fainter the further away she got.

"Why is a child so young as Florence living at the academy, Jesse?" Connie asked.

"Florence's case is an isolated one. Both her parents perished from cholera. There was no one to take young Florence in, and because it was apparent she was blind since birth, the orphanage brought her here." He stopped speaking and shrugged his thin shoulders. "Still, I think it is the better choice for the child's sake. Here, we are as contained as we can be from society. There's a much smaller chance of Florence contracting some nasty illness. At the orphanage," he stopped again and shook his head sadly. "There is such a high rate of illness that claims the lives of so many of the little ones."

Connie placed her hand over her heart and Emma let out a moan.

"The little mite is always getting knocked over by the older children who are trying to find their way in their sightless world."

"That breaks my heart," Connie said, her voice cracking with emotion. "It is also the sad truth that because Florence is blind, she has a very low chance of being adopted."

Sam took her hand and gave it a gentle squeeze.

It was then Mister Caldwell returned.

"Doctor McGreevy? Are you ready to see the doctor's cottage?"

Sam had the distinct feeling that Connie wasn't finished speaking about little Florence, but he knew that he had to look at the cottage and return to Carlyle Street. He was due to start his shift at the bar, and Connie was being collected by Doctor Scopes' private carriage to visit his niece.

And, there was the great importance of speaking with Connie alone about his sudden decision to accept a position at the academy as a physician. She had to be wondering why it was suddenly happening and she knew nothing about it. He needed her to understand that it was something he only came to realize he wanted after visiting the academy, but more importantly, it was also to remain close to her.

They said their farewells to Jesse and were accompanied by Mister Caldwell who retrieved a key to the vacant cottage from his office.

When they exited the academy through the great double doors, light snow was falling.

"Looks like it could be a white Christmas," Mister Caldwell said pulling the collar of his coat up around his ears.

Sam took hold of Connie's arm and was extra careful in guiding her in case of any slippery spots on the cobblestone path to the cottage.

Connie was very quiet, and maybe even a touch sad, and that made Sam nervous. He couldn't just blurt out his plans in front of Mister Caldwell, and he didn't feel comfortable talking about private matters in front of Emma, so he would need to wait and explain everything to her later at dinner.

The cottage was quite cozy.

Sam explained the layout to Connie as they walked through

the cottage.

There was a large entry room with a fireplace with a mantle and an ornate mirror. Wood was already chopped and stacked. Mister Caldwell also mentioned there was a woodshed outside that was full. There were two settees, a large stuffed chair, and a table.

Off the entry room was a kitchen with a sink, larder and stove.

There was a decent-sized bedroom with a bed and two dressers. There was even a small box room next to the bedroom.

"Could be an office," Mister Caldwell said.

Or a nursery, Sam thought to himself.

With marriage on his mind, it wasn't too farfetched to hope a family might not be so far behind. Just seeing the limited interaction between Connie and little Florence was so heartwarming. Connie would be the best mother there ever was.

He only hoped luck stayed on his side.

Chapter 10

❧

"Are you certain that you don't wish me to accompany you?" Emma asked as they waited inside the warm lobby of The Albion and waited for the arrival of Doctor Scopes and his carriage to take Connie to visit his niece, Sophie."

"I will be perfectly fine with Doctor Scopes. I look at this as a duty of mine to perform. To lend my experience and my helping hands to another woman who has lost her sight. I am certain if too many people are around Sophie, she will withdraw further. Trust me, Emma, I know what I am doing."

"I am concerned as well that you haven't eaten lunch. You could become very lightheaded and possibly faint."

Connie was touched by Emma's concern.

"I will be in the capable company of a leading physician. Though I seriously doubt I will faint from lack of food. I come from hardy stock, Emma," Connie said with a touch of laughter in her voice.

"Well, if you're sure..."

Connie squeezed Emma's arm.

"I am perfectly sure. And Emma, I wanted to mention how lovely it was of you to give little Florence your broach. It seemed to make her very happy."

"It was only a small thing. I…I feel so bad for the little one. She is much too young to be among those older children. She gets trampled so easily."

A feeling of despair weighed on Connie's shoulders.

"Yes, I agree. But for right now, it is better than being at the orphanage where she has little chance to thrive."

"Oh, I think I see the carriage and it is splendid! There is a man of perhaps forty years or so and very finely dressed exiting the carriage and heading into the hotel."

"I cannot tell through my heavily veiled vision if it is Doctor Scopes. So, we shall wait until he sees me."

"Connie!"

"That is Doctor Scopes," Connie said.

"Good afternoon, Connie. You look lovely today," Peters said.

"Thank you, Peter. Good afternoon to you, too. Let me introduce my companion, Emma."

"Good afternoon, Emma," he said politely.

"Good afternoon to you, Doctor Scopes."

"Shall we go, Connie? Sophie is aware of your impending arrival. You may join us of course, Emma."

"Connie wishes to go alone to meet with your niece," Emma said.

Connie turned to face Emma.

"You enjoy your afternoon to yourself, Emma. I will be perfectly fine in the capable hands of Doctor Scopes."

***

They discussed Sophie's condition and melancholy on the

ride to the home of Peter's sister, Therese. Connie had the distinct feeling that Peter only knew about Sophie's condition from what his sister told him. That even as a doctor who was so greatly admired by those in his profession and society in general, even he felt awkward, and dare she think *helpless* to help his niece, so he avoided her.

It wasn't at all unusual.

But she was quick to stress that Sophie would not change overnight. There was no formula, amount of speaking, or even crazy stuff like voodoo or witchcraft that could instantly change Sophie's attitude.

Sophie just had to feel it on her own, and when she was ready she would ask for help.

Or not.

It was impossible to know what would happen.

They arrived at the home of Peter Scopes' sister, Missus Therese Morgan. Missus Morgan's husband, Harold, was an importer of some sort and often traveled for business. Sophie was their only child.

Peter had explained this to Connie before their arrival.

He helped Connie from the carriage and she held his arm as he guided her up the steps to the front door of the three-story townhome where the Morgan's resided.

They were met at the door by a housekeeper and ushered into the parlor where Missus Morgan waited.

"Therese, this is Miss Connie Sweet," Peter introduced them.

Missus Morgan took Connie's hand into hers.

"Thank you for visiting us today, Miss Sweet. I am at my wit's end with Sophie."

As with Peter, she hoped Missus Morgan didn't expect a miracle or instant results with Sophie.

"Please call me Connie, Missus Morgan. I am happy to be here to speak with your daughter. Please understand this is a process, and Sophie will likely resist anything I have to say to her today. We can only hope that in time, she will accept her condition and come around enough to allow others to help her to help herself."

"It's Therese," she said giving Connie's hand a gentle squeeze, "and I am just grateful for anything you might be able to do for my daughter."

"Well, I will do my very best. Please take me to her."

"Connie, I will be waiting in the parlor for you. But please take all the time you need," Peter said.

"I...I don't know what to do," Therese said awkwardly. "I mean...to help you...Connie. To get upstairs."

It was very apparent that Therese Morgan felt as helpless and almost hopeless as her brother did, even more so. She wanted to help, but she didn't know how to help or even realize most of what was needed from her as a mother to a newly blind child was common sense.

"If you could just lead me upstairs to Sophie's quarters, that will be just fine. Once I am familiar with a place, I learn very quickly where things are and how to get around without bumping into things or knocking things over."

She hoped she came across to Therese as confident and at ease with the situation.

"Yes, of course."

Therese led her up the stairs and down a hallway. She knocked twice on a door and opened it.

"Sophie, Connie is here to speak with you. You must listen to what she has to say. I will have tea sent up."

Connie could hear the exasperation in Therese's voice.

That only made things worse for Sophie.

Yet at the same time, she understood Therese's position as well.

"Thank you, Therese," Connie said politely.

"Would either of you like some biscuits or perhaps something more substantial to eat?" Therese asked.

"Tea would be lovely, Therese."

Connie noticed that Sophie didn't utter a word.

When Therese left the room, Connie had to strain her very limited vision to find Sophie. Therese had forgotten already that Connie's sight was impaired. Luckily, Connie could make out shapes and light coming in through a window. In front of the window was an overstuffed chair with a woman sitting on it, her legs drawn up beneath her.

Connie felt her way to where Sophie sat and sat across from her on an empty wing chair.

"Hello, Sophie. I'm Connie. I'm happy to meet you."

After what seemed like minutes of achingly long silence, a small voice replied. "Hello."

One single word.

But it was a start.

"Sophie, please know that I am so very, very sorry that you have lost your sight. I know that my saying this means little to you, but as your mother and your uncle have told you, I, too, have lost my sight. It was not sudden, as yours was, but we do share the same unfortunate outcome. As young adults, our vision was taken from us."

"So you are here to tell me it all gets better? That I will survive in darkness?"

There was a definite anger in her voice.

Connie knew that anger well.

She, too, experienced rage and anger when her vision failed.

"You have every right to be angry, Sophie. What has happened to you isn't fair. You did nothing wrong. But you can live a normal life again. It will just be a different life. Still, you can thrive and accomplish many things."

"You sound like one of those letters that my mother has read to me from blind girl schools."

"Well, I am the product of one of those blind girl schools. Only I am here to help you if you'll allow me to. I am not here to drag you off to some school or to make money from your parents."

"What you have failed to mention, Connie is that you still have *some* sight. My uncle says so."

"Your uncle is correct. I have limited vision. I compare it to standing in a very deep fog. I can make out shapes, I can see light and dark. On a very good day, even a little color. But the difference between you and I is that yes, you are completely blind. I am not totally blind, but I live in the knowledge every single day and every single night that I could wake up and be totally blind. That is always on my mind, Sophie. I don't take for granted what I have, for I know I could lose it in an instant."

Once again, silence enveloped the room.

"Sophie, I can teach you the basics of living life as a blind woman. I can share with you my experiences of being blind. I can also assure you that with time, patience, and effort, you can function in society to a nearly normal degree, as I do."

"I don't think that is possible for me," Sophie said sadly.

"Why not? I wanted to become a teacher, and I have. If I can fall in love with a man that loves me back, then so can you. I fully intend to be a wife and a mother. I go out to dinner, I go to the theater, I go to the opera. I have a very supportive family, just as you do. My family was as shocked and didn't know how to react when I lost my sight. Just as your family is now. But you are very lucky, as I was, that our families have the means to provide a stellar education in life as a blind woman. Your family also has the means to provide you with a companion to accompany you outside the home."

"Is the man you love blind?" She asked.

"No, he is fully sighted and he is a new doctor. As a matter of fact, he is accepting a position at the blind academy here in town."

"That is nice for you, I suppose."

"Yes, it is. Let me tell you a little secret, Sophie. Years ago, my Auntie Minerva visited this very town and stayed in the same hotel as I am currently staying on the wonderful Carlyle Street. Most unexpectedly, Auntie Minerva met the man she would eventually marry. She told me this town, and Carlyle Street is magical. I wanted to believe that, and that is the reason I accepted the teaching position at the blind academy. And do you know what? I met Sam the very night I arrived in this town. Let the magic work for you, too, Sophie."

"Sounds like some fairy story, Connie."

"A fairy story come to life, Sophie. It can happen. If it happened to me, it can happen to you, too. You have to want it."

"If I'm shipped off to some fancy blind girl school, it won't happen."

Connie thought for a moment.

"What if you try spending some time at the blind academy? I will be there everyday teaching, and I will be living there. So you will know someone. And you could return home every day if you choose. You can start small, and learn the basics with the other girls. There are girls there who are a bit younger than you, some are fifteen and sixteen years of age, but the goal is the same – to learn to become self-sufficient."

"I don't know," she said warily.

"Well, you have a think about it. If you want to visit the school, I will happy to accompany you. If you would rather have private lessons here in your home, I will teach you. Maybe after Christmas when the crowds have gone away, we can venture out together to Carlyle Street."

***

Connie took a late lunch with Doctor Peter Scopes at a small eatery on Carlyle Street. Since the lunch rush was over, they were able to be seated right away.

"I can't thank you enough for visiting with Sophie," Peter spoke after they ordered their meals.

"I am happy to help if I can. Sophie is naturally resistant to everything I have offered. I hope in time, she will accept my help. Right now, she is still mourning the loss of her vision, and to her, it feels like the loss of her life. She is also angry, and justifiably so."

"Her parents don't know what more they can do. I hate seeing them all suffer so much. That is why I am so incredibly grateful that you agreed to visit Sophie. I also am so thankful that you spent so much time afterward with my sister, explaining things to her that I don't think she ever realized or considered. It's all a great help."

Connie felt around for her teacup and carefully took a sip.

"Sophie just has to feel it, Peter. Once she can find her way beyond her rage and the sorrow, she will be ready to make that next step. I am hoping that she will take in an afternoon of shopping with me after the holidays. And, as I explained to you

103

and your sister, while I know our local blind academy is not the most prominent or best-equipped educational facility for the blind, I can attest that the staff is supportive and full of love and the facility is clean and cared for. Sophie could spend a few hours a week there with me, learning skills with the older girls that are there."

"I think it is a marvelous idea, Connie. It could give Sophie the confidence she needs to venture out to a boarding school, perhaps even the school you attended. If you would be kind enough to recommend her."

"Absolutely, Peter," she answered at once.

"In the meantime, is there anything at all that I can do for you?

Connie thought about Sam, Emma and about the blind academy.

"Yes, yes there is, Peter. I could really use your help this afternoon."

"Anything, Connie. Just name it."

Chapter 11

C onnie returned to The Albion at four in the afternoon. It had been quite a day.

After her lunch with Doctor Peter Scopes, he accompanied her to Carlyle Street to assist her in shopping.

Their first stop was the butcher shop.

Here, Connie ordered several very large smoked hams to be delivered to the blind academy. Peter sent mutton, rabbit, and chickens to the academy for Christmas lunch and dinner.

They then visited the greengrocer.

Connie ordered pounds of potatoes, and twenty pounds each of carrots, and parsnips to be delivered to the blind academy. Peter took care of ordering apples, pears, and dried fruit for the academy.

At the bakery, fruit cakes and fruit biscuits were ordered for the teachers, doctors, staff, and of course, the children. Coffee, tea, and chocolate for hot drinks were also being gifted.

They then practically cleared out the toy shop of its stock for the children at the academy. Toy trains, dolls, and other tactile items to stimulate their young minds would be wrapped and delivered to the academy before Christmas.

And then it was time for more personal gifts.

For Sam, a pair of gold cufflinks with his initials were purchased and wrapped. Peter wired an order to a medical supply store in the next county for the delivery of a top-of-the-line stethoscope and other items for Sam's doctor's bag.

For Emma, three new day dresses and a pair of sturdy but fashionable shoes for her new position at the blind academy as a teacher's aide. At the leather goods shop, Connie purchased a large durable leather travel bag for Emma. She also purchased a gold locket pendant as a special thank you for all the assistance she had provided to Connie since her arrival at The Albion.

She also purchased a roundtrip first-class train ticket for Emma to return home to celebrate Christmas with her family before she returned and began her employment as a teacher's aide at the blind academy.

For Florence, there were dolls, pull toys, dresses, nighties, stockings, hair bows, and everything imaginable for the little perfect girl who Connie couldn't get off her mind since meeting her at the blind academy that morning.

Connie had already resolved that she would be assuming care of Florence at the blind academy just like she was her own daughter. She could keep her near her at all times and safe so she wasn't trampled or injured anymore by the other rambunctious children. She planned to ask for a cot to be placed in her room for Florence.

After a short rest, Emma arrived and helped her dress in anticipation of her dinner with Sam.

It was then she presented Emma with her gifts and the train tickets home.

At once, Emma burst into tears.

"No one has ever been so good to me, Connie! I love you so much! I am so grateful."

Connie hugged her friend. "This is just a token of my affection and appreciation for your friendship and for all you have done for me. I am the one who is grateful. Now dry those tears!"

Emma obediently removed a handkerchief from her dress pocket and wiped her eyes.

"Sam is going to ask you to marry him."

"Oh, Emma…" Connie's cheeks heated. "I don't know about that."

"What will you say if he asks you to marry him?" Emma pressed on.

Connie didn't mind indulging in a bit of personal talk with Emma, but talking about Sam possibly asking her to marry him didn't feel right.

Especially if he didn't ask.

"I can't answer that, Emma. I mean, I do love Sam, but if it happens, I will decide then."

"He took a job at the blind academy to be near you. I am sure that is the reason. I heard that he had planned to speak to Mister Anderton's friend, Doctor Larsen, about possibly working at the coroner's office."

"Oh?" Connie asked coyly. "Well, perhaps he was caught up in the moment while at the blind academy this morning. I am not certain he has officially been offered and has accepted a position."

In truth, Sam had discussed with her the possibility of seeking a position in the coroner's office. That was the reason she was so shocked when he suddenly asked to see the medical facilities at the blind academy as well as a vacant cottage set aside on the grounds of the academy for doctors working on the premises. She planned to speak about it at dinner tonight with Sam.

Luckily, the subject veered away from Sam and potential marriage proposals to Emma's new job at the academy. She had put in her notice to leave her kitchen position at The Albion. She planned to move into her room at the blind academy before the new year.

"Miss Lily seemed relieved that I was leaving kitchen service."

Connie could hear the touch of humor in Emma's voice.

"I am sure they will miss you in the kitchen," Connie said even though Miss Lily and the other kitchen staff girls probably were relieved that Emma was leaving The Albion.

"They are happy for me that I have a new job that I am happy about, and they are also happy there will be no more broken dishes and burned food in The Albion's kitchen," Emma said as she placed a feathered ornament against Connie's hair and pinned it into place with matching pearl hairpins.

"I'm sure that is true that they are happy about your new exciting position at the blind academy. You will need to keep them updated because I have a feeling that you will progress quickly and be a teacher in no time."

***

Sam quickly left his room at The Albion and descended the back staircase to the lobby where he was to meet his beloved Connie.

With Christmas so close and the hotel full, he hadn't had a minute's break at the hotel bar, and he didn't get to leave on time because there were just so many patrons at the bar and not enough staff in place.

The crowd finally thinned out with the patrons either going

out for the evening for dinner and shopping or settling into their rooms before heading down to the hotel's restaurant, which is where Sam was taking Connie for dinner. Sam rushed upstairs for a quick wash and change of clothing.

Connie was already waiting for him on one of the velvet chairs in the hotel's lobby.

For a moment, he stopped and took in just how beautiful she was. She wore a lovely blue frock, her hair was perfect and she just…shone. Even in the harsh light of the hotel lobby, she was a ray of sunshine.

And he loved her!

He loved her so much and wanted to spend the rest of his life with her.

If she would have him.

He weaved through the guests until he reached her.

"I'm sorry, Connie. I am late." He touched her hand.

"I have been sitting here just enjoying the sound of people coming and going. So even if you are a minute or two late, it isn't important. I am here, and you are here now. That is what is important."

And with those few words, once again, Sam McGreevy was awash with love for this woman.

"We have reservations at the hotel restaurant. Afterward I thought we would have a browse on Carlyle Street since all the shops are open late tonight for last-minute gift buying."

He helped her to her feet, and she took his arm.

"That sounds like a wonderful plan, Sam."

The hotel restaurant was still crowded, but as soon as the hostess spotted him, they were led to a small table near a window. Sam ordered a pot of tea for two, and then helped Connie with her chair, and then took a seat across from her.

"Is there anything special you would like to eat this evening, Connie? Or shall I read the menu to you?"

"While I was sitting in the lobby, I overheard a woman say that the roast pheasant with the almond and potato pudding, followed by the tray of currant drop biscuits was simply delightful."

"That sounds very good, Connie. I will have the same."

After their order was taken, and the tea was poured by Connie, she asked, "Tell me, Sam, about what happened at the blind academy. Did you really accept a position as a doctor?"

Pride filled his heart.

Connie was smiling at him.

"Yes, Connie, I accepted a position as a doctor. I will be moving into the cottage they assigned to me right after Christmas. I am most anxious to begin my career."

"Is there any special reason you chose to work with the blind? I know that it's not as prestigious or well-paying as perhaps the position you spoke of at the coroner's office."

"Well, Dear Connie, I was truly moved by the tour of the facility this morning. I had this very strong feeling come over me that the blind academy was where I needed to be. I feel like I need it, as much as it needs me." He then paused and added, "And of course, it allows me to be near the woman I love so very, very much." The words, *Will you marry me, Constance Sweet* almost left his lips. But the busy restaurant at The Albion Hotel was not the perfect place to propose marriage.

"I think that makes your first job as a doctor a very special one."

"Oh, I couldn't agree more." He then asked, "What did you think of the blind academy, Connie? It was your first time being there as well. Was it everything you imagined from the letters you exchanged with Mister Caldwell?"

"Actually, no it wasn't, Sam."

Sam was sure at that moment his heart dropped into his stomach.

"It was a lot better than I expected."

And just like that, he was happy again.

And relieved.

For a few seconds, his mind had traveled to dark places. Connie returning to her parents' home and never seeing her again.

"There is something I wanted to tell you, Sam. Something I decided."

This time, his stomach lurched.

"It's about Florence."

The delightful three-year-old living at the blind academy.

His stomach relaxed.

"Yes, Connie?"

"I haven't been able to get Florence off my mind since we left her behind at the academy." Connie raised her hand to her heart. "I know we promised to visit on Christmas day, and I bought her so many Christmas gifts today, and for the other children, too, of course, as well as food."

"That is so lovely of you, Connie. I am sure the children will appreciate it so much. I had little Florence on my mind as well."

"I have done some thinking, and I fell in love with Florence immediately, and she seemed to take to me very quickly as well…"

"It was very apparent that the two of you became quick friends."

"Yes, well, I have decided that since I am a single woman and therefore not permitted to adopt, I plan to take Florence under my wing, so to speak. Keep her close to me at all times at the academy, and I am going to ask to have her cot moved to my room. I wish to be as much of a mother as I can to her since she has no living parents, and while it is honorable that the staff at the blind academy has taken her in, she is too young to be immersed in all the students. I will be the one who teaches Florence everything she needs to know to become a fully functioning blind child, and later, God willing, a blind woman."

This woman he loved, never failed to fascinate him with her goodness.

Then the words tumbled out of his mouth.

"Connie, will you marry me? I want nothing more than to be your husband and a father to Florence. We will adopt her. She will be our daughter."

"Yes, Sam. I will marry you. I love you. I knew when I arrived on Carlyle Street and met you that first night, something special was about to happen, and now it has."

Her smile was radiant. For the first time in his life, Sam McGreevy felt he was a whole person. He had a career, he had a family, and finally, he found love. Not just a wife who he would treasure, but a beautiful little daughter as well.

He reached across the table and took her hand.

"I love you, too, Connie. I knew as well that I wanted to marry you the moment I first saw you that night. Things have never been better in my life. The blessings keep coming. You, Florence, passed my exams, and my first job as a doctor. Even before becoming a doctor, I have always wanted a family of my own."

"Can I tell you something?" She asked coyly.

"Of course. Anything."

"My Auntie Minerva, who was to accompany me to The Albion to spend some girl time together shopping…"

"Yes, she wasn't able to come, unfortunately. But the good news is her twin babies are full of health once more," he added.

"Indeed! God is good! But Auntie Minerva told me the story of how she met her husband. She had traveled to Carlyle Street at Christmas time a few years ago. On her own, as I did. She was shopping and going to the theatre, and all the wonderful things Carlyle Street has to offer. But here at The Albion, she met her soon-to-be husband. She was coming back from an early morning of shopping and her pearl necklace that was passed down to her from her grandmother broke, sending all the pearls scattering onto the floor. She told me she was practically in tears until this wonderful man who was leaving the hotel to purchase a newspaper, stopped and helped her find every precious pearl. After which, they came to this very restaurant and got to know each other over hot cocoa and teacakes." She gave Sam's hand a gentle squeeze.

They fell in love instantly, Sam. Auntie Minerva told me that Carlyle Street and The Albion are magical places. I believe her."

"That is a beautiful story, Connie. I believe too. I believe history has repeated itself. Whether it be Fate, luck, the grace of God, or even this hotel." He gestured around with his hand. "Or even Carlyle Street. I believe." He returned the gentle squeeze to his hand with one of his own for emphasis. "I promise you, Connie, that we are going to be so happy together and so successful that everyone will be in awe of us and our little family with Florence."

Chapter 12

~⁓᪥⁓~

Christmas Eve

Connie Sweet knew she was unwelcome the moment she entered the home of Mister and Missus McGreevy, Sam's parents.

She could tell the house was full of people and noise.

It was also full of smoke, general uncleanliness, and animal smells.

She wanted to leave immediately, but because she loved Sam, and this was his family, she said nothing.

She and Sam had planned to stop by the house so Connie could meet his parents, and deliver the Christmas gifts they had purchased for his family. They then would travel to Thaddeus Anderton's home for a Christmas Eve get-together.

Sam introduced his mother to her in the front room where so many people were moving about.

"It's lovely to meet you, Missus McGreevy," Connie said politely. She took a few steps and stumbled, nearly falling to the floor before Sam caught her at the last minute.

"Are you okay, Connie?" He asked frantically.

"I'm fine, Sam. I'm perfectly fine," she said, even though she was far from it. Her heart was beating double time in her chest. She was completely mortified that she almost fell in front of Sam's mother.

Instead of responding, Missus McGreevy requested her son help her in the kitchen.

"Go along, Sam, I will be fine."

He led her to a hardback chair, and she sat. He pressed a kiss against her forehead. "I will be back momentarily."

Even through the noise of the people in the house, Connie could clearly hear the conversation between Sam and his mother.

Maybe his mother spoke loudly because it was in her nature, or perhaps she actually wanted Connie to overhear her. Most likely, though, it was that Missus McGreevy had not a clue that most blind people have very keen hearing. When the sense of sight vanishes, the sense of hearing steps up to take its place to the best of its ability.

"What do you mean you are going to work at the blind asylum?" Missus McGreevy practically shrieked. "All that money spent on your education so you can make pennies! It's the girl bewitching you, Samuel!"

"First of all, Mother, it is the blind *academy*. I did not become a doctor for the money. To me, I became a doctor to alleviate the suffering of others!"

"Alleviate the suffering of others!" She mocked. "Now that you're a doctor you get to use all your fancy words."

"Yes, Mother, that is why I became a doctor. As for all the money spent, that money came from my wages and the medical

115

school's charity. I was only able to attend because Mister Anderton granted me free room and board at the hotel and a decent wage. He was understanding enough to allow me to perform my work around my school schedule. I could not live here! You have an entire house of layabouts and that is your choice to endure. I am sorry that I cannot hold my tongue like my spineless father who will be driven to an early grave between his fondness for cheap gin and trying to support everyone living here.

And finally, and most importantly, Connie is the love of my life. She is so far above me that I can't believe she has agreed to marry me."

Connie wanted so badly at that moment to go to Sam, to be with him, but she did not want to interfere.

"That's ridiculous, Sam! And when did you get so surly? It's that hotel and being among those rats! As for the girl, just because she comes from wealth means nothing. I'm more concerned for the girl," her voice suddenly lowered and softened. "Think of her. Look at how she stumbled. Can you imagine having children with her? She would drop a baby right on its head! How long will she be happy with someone like you, Sam? She should be with someone like your professor, who is he? Doctor Stope? He's wealthy beyond belief, and I happened to be on Carlyle Street yesterday and saw the two of them about and he was holding her arm!"

"Her name is Connie, Mother. Not *the girl*. If you can't address her with respect, then you won't see us ever again."

At that very moment, something inside Connie Sweet snapped.

She rose from the chair and through her foggy vision, found her way into the kitchen.

"Connie…" Sam began.

She lifted a hand to halt him.

"Missus McGreevy, with all due respect, if you wish to speak about me, whether it be good or bad, you may do it in my presence. I feel that there are things I need to say and that you need to hear and to understand."

Sam's arm took her arm.

It was his silent sign of solidarity with her.

"First of all, I realize that you have no knowledge of the blind. So I will try to be kind. I stumbled inside your home because I am not familiar with the surroundings. There are many people and animals walking and running about. It sometimes takes me a bit of time to acclimate to new surroundings.

Second, yes, I do come from a family of means. Because of this, I was given the finest education possible for me to be able to adapt to becoming a confident blind woman. That is why I have accepted a teaching position at the blind academy – because I feel the desire to pass on my knowledge to others who are blind and whose families cannot pay for a stellar education.

As for my dropping my future children on their heads, I am not crippled or a lunatic. I am more than capable of taking care of any children that I may birth or who are in my care. Better than most mothers, I assure you.

If you need the truth about your spotting me out and about with Doctor Scopes, not Stope, I had an appointment with him and his sister to visit with his newly blinded niece. Sam was well aware of this. Afterward, Doctor Scopes was kind enough to accompany me to Carlyle Street so that I could shop for Christmas gifts for Sam, and my friend, Emma. He also helped me to arrange deliveries of meat, vegetables, and toys to the blind academy for Christmas, and he is so generous that he also sent a large quantity of food to the blind academy. He is a good man, and he is also old enough to be my father.

And finally, I am sorry if you feel that I am not good enough for your son and that I somehow lured him into accepting his first employment as a doctor at the blind academy. I love your son, and I know he loves me. I am very sorry if you cannot accept that."

"Let's go, Connie. I don't want to be here any longer," Sam practically spat out the words. "Merry Christmas, Mother. I hope you enjoy the gifts that Connie and I have brought for you and the family. Please tell Papa whenever he drags himself home from the tavern that I wish him a Merry Christmas as well."

He led Connie from the kitchen and through the maze of bodies in motion. Some people were speaking to Sam, but he kept moving to the door, and they walked straight from the house and onto the street.

They walked in silence until they were halfway between Sam's family home and Carlyle Street. Finally, Sam halted and turned to Connie who was trying to hold her emotions in check.

He took both of her hands into his.

"Your hands are so cold, Connie! I am so very sorry for taking you to my family home and I am so sorry for how my mother spoke about you."

His words and the soft, hurt tone in his voice caused tears to rise in her eyes.

"I am sorry that your mother doesn't like me, Sam. I would fully understand if you don't want to marry me."

"No! No! No! Connie! Please don't think that! I love you more than life itself. My mother…my family, is driven by the constant need for money. It's not you that she is upset over.

She is upset over the possibility that I won't make a fortune by working at the blind academy, and therefore I won't elevate them from the poverty that they have created for themselves."

"It is me, too. Your mother believes that I lured you into accepting a job at the blind academy."

"That is so untrue, Connie. My mother doesn't understand that my motives for becoming a doctor were to alleviate the suffering of others. Yes, money is a consideration. But as long as I have enough to provide for you and Florence comfortably, that is all I am concerned with."

"She is so angry, Sam." Connie slowly shook her head.

"And I don't want either of us anywhere near that anger. She will come around and accept things as they will be and apologize to you, or she can stay out of our lives. I cannot have that kind of presence around us or around Florence."

Light snow began to fall. Connie couldn't see it, but she could feel the little individual flakes drop onto her hair and face.

"Now, Connie, let us go back to the hotel and change clothing. I feel like my clothes stink from that house. We shall get ready and then I will hail us a carriage and we will be off to Thaddeus' home to celebrate Christmas Eve with people who will welcome us."

***

Sam changed from the old sack suit that he used to wear to medical school and tossed it into a corner of his hotel room.

He would never wear it again.

But he would not throw it away or burn it. No, the suit had been left behind by someone who had stayed at The Albion. Sam would see to it that the suit was laundered and given to someone else who needed it.

His nostrils were still filled with the smell of smoke and the uncleanliness of his family home.

Many times in his life, he had been embarrassed by his home, his family members, and his lack of money. But for Connie to actually be among all that he loathed, and for his mother to treat Connie so poorly, he first felt nothing but anger.

Now the anger had morphed into sadness and that same embarrassment of the past.

What had he been thinking?

He should have known how his mother would react to not only his engagement to Connie but to his accepting a job at the blind academy as well.

Blind.

Yes, that was the word.

Not Connie's blindness.

His mother's blindness.

Blinded by the want of money and comfort.

Blinded by her prejudice to Connie, because she perceived Connie not to be perfect because she had lost most of her sight.

But at that moment, as he stood now fully dressed in his sharp black suit and staring into the old cracked mirror in his hotel room, he decided that he would not allow himself to be blinded.

Blinded by the anger he felt.

Blinded by the sadness he felt.

Blinded by the embarrassment he felt.

No, he would not.

By allowing those emotions to take hold of him, then he would lose his joy.

And joy had taken so long to come to him.

The joy of finding the love of his life.

Of her agreeing to marry him.

His Connie.

The joy of little Florence coming into their lives.

Of officially becoming a doctor.

Something he worked so long and so hard for.

For new friends like Thaddeus Anderton, who accepted him into his world without a second thought.

Joy overtook everything else.

And Sam only wanted joy and love in his life.

***

Connie was waiting for him in the lobby. There weren't very many people about.

When he saw her, his heart flipped, just as it always did. He loved her so much.

She was wearing her coat and a white fur hat and matching gloves. On her lap were the gifts they had purchased for Thaddeus and Miss Lily, Thaddeus' companion.

She looked beautiful, but she also looked sad.

And that pained his heart.

He walked quickly to her.

"Connie, my darling, you look beautiful! Are you ready to go?"

She smiled, but he was sure it wasn't genuine.

"Yes, I am ready."

"Let me ask the doorman to hail a coach and we will be on our way."

The doorman wasn't more than a few minutes when he walked back into the hotel and waved to Sam.

Sam was juggling the assorted wrapped gifts in his arms while trying to help Connie to her feet. It must have looked comical or pathetic, depending on who might have witnessed the spectacle. The doorman rushed over and took the gifts from Sam, and Sam was able to help Connie to her feet and led her from the hotel.

"It's going to snow later this evening," the doorman said as he loaded the gifts into the coach. Everyone is saying it could be a very white Christmas."

Sam tipped the doorman. He didn't know the man personally. He must have been a new hire at The Albion.

Once they were safely inside, the coach moved and made its way to Thaddeus Anderton's home. They were quiet during the ride. Sam was nervous about going to Thaddeus' home. Doctor Scopes' party was a major event, but somehow to Sam, this event was even more exciting because it was a reinforcement that Thaddeus saw Sam as more or less an equal now.

When the coach slowed to a stop, Connie finally spoke.

"Sam, if you don't mind, I would like the coachman to take me back to the hotel. I am not up for socializing this evening. But you stay and enjoy yourself."

He took her gloved hand into his.

He knew this was about the terrible experience at his parents' home.

"Please come with me, Connie. I am sure we will have a wonderful evening. It won't be anything like what happened at my parents' home. I am so sorry that my mother hurt your feelings."

After a few moments of silence, Connie spoke again.

"Yes, I understand that, Sam. Still, I would rather return to the hotel."

"Okay," he agreed. "Let me go inside and tell Thaddeus that we won't be staying and I will leave the gifts."

"You don't have to return with me, Sam. You should enjoy yourself with your friends."

"Absolutely not. I love you and I will return to the hotel with you. We will have a nice dinner at the hotel restaurant and we can talk about our upcoming wedding and Florence, and going to the blind academy tomorrow for Christmas."

She nodded and he dropped a light kiss against her forehead.

He hopped down from the coach. The coachman was waiting.

"I will be back momentarily. I need to speak to the home-owner, and then we will be returning to The Albion."

"Very good, Sir."

Sam walked to the front door of the incredibly large home of Thaddeus Anderton. At the moment, he vowed someday he would purchase a home just like this one for his own family.

He knocked, and a maid opened the door. The sounds of people talking and laughing poured out the open doorway. It was obvious the party was already going strong.

"Good evening, could you let Mister Anderton know that Sam McGreevy needs to speak with him?"

"Would you like to come in, Sir?" she asked.

"No, but thank you."

She took the gifts from his arms and walked back through the foyer of the home.

A few minutes later, Thaddeus appeared in the foyer.

"Why are you still outside, Sam?" he asked.

"I am sorry, Thaddeus, Connie isn't feeling very festive this evening."

Miss Lily walked up beside Thaddeus and took his arm. As always, she was dressed in white. Sam didn't know the extent of their relationship, he only heard rumors at the hotel. Miss Lily seemed to have become Thaddeus' companion. That in itself was interesting since it was well-known that Thaddeus was a confirmed bachelor. But, Sam knew from his own falling in love with Connie, that when the right woman comes along into a man's life, he is powerless to resist.

"Is she ill?" Thaddeus asked.

"No, we had a rather unpleasant exchange with my mother earlier. I believe Connie is still very sad and shaken. She is waiting in the coach. We are going to return to the hotel."

"Oh no!" Lily exclaimed. "Thaddeus, let us talk to Connie and change her mind."

Lily walked from the house with Thaddeus directly behind her. Sam followed.

Thaddeus opened the carriage door and helped Lily up into the coach where she took a seat beside Connie.

"Connie, it is Lily and Thaddeus is here as well. Sam told us you want to go back to the hotel, that his mother upset you."

"It was unpleasant, Lily, yes. But I have encouraged Sam to stay and enjoy the festivities."

"Please join us, Connie. You will have a much more enjoyable evening with us than you will at the hotel," Lily encouraged. "Besides, even if Sam stayed, I am certain he would not have a good time without you."

"I wouldn't want to put a damper on your festivities."

Sam's heart hurt at Connie's words. It pained him to know how upset his beloved Connie was.

"Nonsense, Connie! Why don't you come inside for a bit and have something to eat and drink, and if you still feel the same way, my driver will take you and Sam back to the hotel," Thaddeus offered.

Connie nodded.

"Yes, you are both correct. I shouldn't let one unpleasant exchange ruin my night or Sam's night."

"Wonderful!" Thaddeus thundered.

Sam helped Connie from the coach, and immediately, Lily

took charge and looped her arm through Connie's arm and gave her a small hug. "Let's get out of this cold, Connie. The clouds are angry! They are going to open up and spill out all their snow!" Lily said dramatically.

Sam was relieved that Thaddeus and Miss Lily had come to the rescue.

Once inside, Lily helped Connie out of her coat and hat and at admired everything about Connie and what she was wearing.

From the festive red and green dress to the fancy black silk shoes, to the red pearl hair pins. Lily couldn't stop with her compliments.

A maid took Sam's coat and hat, another took away Connie's outer garments, and yet another offered them refreshments.

Thaddeus then escorted Sam and Connie into the parlor where the guests had gathered around the fire.

"Doctor Sam McGreevy and Miss Connie Sweet," Thaddeus began. "This is John Tavish, judge. Vicar Clausen. We don't call him Vicar outside of the church, just *Claus.*"

Everyone let out a laugh.

"Everitt Singleton, my lawyer. Andrew Parker and Missus Ann Parker, own the town newspaper.

"Doctor Anton Larsen and his wife Rosey."

Sam recognized the name of the town coroner.

Rosey Larsen stood and walked to Connie and took her hand.

"I'm Rosey. I am Lily's sister and dear friend of Thaddeus. It's delightful to meet you, Connie."

"Wonderful to meet you, Rosey," Connie said with a smile.

This smile though was genuine, Sam knew.

They were now among friends.

"Peter Scopes and a few other guests will be along shortly after their previous commitments," Thaddeus added.

Sam settled on a plush settee beside Connie, and a butler brought a small table into the parlor and set it in front of Connie, followed by a maid who placed a china cup of tea on the table for Connie.

"I hope the table makes it easier for you, Connie," Thaddeus said.

"Thank you for being so thoughtful. The table is a great help," Connie said.

Sam was silently grateful for everyone accommodating Connie's needs. Sam knew she could get by fine on her own, but it was touching that everyone was trying to assist her.

It was easy after that.

With everyone being so friendly and interesting, Connie seemed to settle into the conversation. Sam was in awe at how she took such a genuine interest in each person who spoke to her. He could only hope that it distracted her from the ugliness of earlier when she met his family.

Just the thought of what happened caused a horrible acidic feeling to wash over him.

"So, what do you two have planned for Christmas?" Lily asked.

"Sam and I will be going to the blind academy to visit the children."

"How lovely!" Lily exclaimed.

Sam reached over and took Connie's hand into his. "Shall we tell everyone our news?"

Connie smiled and immediately his heart warmed.

"News? We can all use good news," Thaddeus said.

"You tell them," Sam encouraged Connie.

"Sam and I are to marry as soon as possible. We are also planning to adopt a little girl at the blind academy named

Florence who has stolen both of our hearts. She is three years old."

The room erupted with applause and shouts of good wishes.

"Little Florence should be here with us," Thaddeus said.

"It would be wonderful, but I don't think Mister Caldwell, who runs the academy, would be very accommodating to remove Florence from the academy this evening, especially since Connie and I are not yet married."

"Nonsense!" Thaddeus bellowed. "I know Caldwell. We have a judge and a vicar present right in the very room. You two can marry right now by our good judge, and have the marriage blessed at morning service by Claus."

Sam's heart began to beat double, then triple time in his chest.

"Connie, is this something you would like?" Sam asked.

Silently, he prayed she would agree.

"Yes, I would love to get married here in this wonderful home surrounded by friends."

He leaned over and kissed her cheek.

"Connie, I have the most perfect dress for you to wear to church in the morning," Lily added.

"Thank you, thank you, everyone!" Connie said sincerely.

"Yes, thank you to you all for helping our new life together to begin," Sam added.

Chapter 13

❦

The party progressed quickly from a Christmas gathering to an impromptu wedding.

Connie's head was spinning.

Thaddeus Anderton had a telephone in his home. Though it took some time, Connie was able to call her parents and receive their blessing. Though it was sad they would not be there to see their daughter married, they would visit at the start of the new year.

The judge took his carriage to the town clerk's office and obtained the marriage book so the marriage would be official. While he was at the office, he would send a wire to Mister Caldwell that Florence should be ready to be collected within the next hour. They would have the marriage blessed during the Christmas service in the morning. The vicar's wife assured Connie that the church was fully decorated in flowers and looking its most stunning.

Hopefully, through some magic of Thaddeus Anderton and Lily, a wedding ring for Connie would be procured. If not, they would visit the jeweler the day after Christmas.

The ring was an important symbol, but it was the wedding vows that counted the most. In just a short time she would be not only a wife but a mother as well. The responsibility would be great, but something Connie was more than prepared for.

They stood together before the grand fireplace in Thaddeus Anderton's grand home. Connie could even make out some of the details of the ornate fireplace in her limited vision.

Lily stood beside her and Thaddeus beside Sam as they exchanged vows surrounded by their new friends. Even Peter Scopes managed to arrive at the very last minute before the impromptu ceremony.

It was beautiful.

It was meaningful.

It was real.

And most importantly, she loved Sam, and Sam loved her.

It was that simple.

When Judge Tavish proclaimed them man and wife, Sam's lips gently touched hers.

Once again, the home erupted in applause and congratulations. Everyone hugged them and wished them a lifetime of happiness and health.

"Now, let's go and fetch your Florence before the snow really comes down," Thaddeus suggested.

"Would you like to stay behind and warm?" Sam asked.

"No, I feel I should come along. Florence may be a bit frightened and disoriented."

"Yes, of course, my darling, you are right."

Lily and her sister Rosey helped Connie with her coat, hat, and gloves.

"We will have a bedroom set up for you all to stay in tonight,"

Lily said.

"We don't want to impose…"

"You are not imposing. Thaddeus and I are delighted to have the company," she insisted. "Claus and his wife will go to The Albion and collect Florence's gifts that you bought for her. That way she will have new clothing to change into."

"I can't thank you all enough," Connie said sincerely.

"And I second that," Sam added. "Now let's go and get our girl."

***

"Miss Connie, are you my mama now?"

Sam watched the first interaction of mother and daughter with misty eyes.

Connie held Florence in her arms, they were cheek to cheek.

"Yes, I am your mama now, and Sam is your papa. That is if you want us as your mama and papa?"

"Oh yes, I needs me a mama and papa," Florence said in her adorable baby voice that melted Sam's heart.

He knew without a doubt, that voice would always melt his heart.

Mister Caldwell and his wife, Missus Caldwell, had prepared Florence for their arrival. She was dressed and had her little coat and hat already on. A small suitcase was at the door.

Judge Tavish signed a few papers. Sam signed another paper. Thaddeus instructed Mister Caldwell to contact his attorney for any other paperwork that might be needed to finalize the adoption.

And just like that, it was time to return to the home of Thaddeus Anderton and continue their celebrations.

With a promise to return to the academy the next day for Christmas, and a request by Sam to have the cottage for his little family ready to move into, they bade the Caldwells goodbye.

Sam took Florence from Connie and held his free arm out for Connie.

This would be a common occurrence for the family of three.

Judge Tavish carried Florence's little suitcase, and they made their way back to Thaddeus' home.

Before going inside, Sam held Florence and explained to her all about the snow that was coming down around them. Finally, Lily looked out the door.

"Sam, bring that baby inside so we can spoil her!" Lily called.

And spoiled she was.

And spoiled, she would always be.

Lovingly spoiled.

Chapter 14

⚜

Christmas Morning

Even though Connie was already married to Sam in the eyes of the law, marrying Sam, and saying the vows again, this time in the eyes of God and a full congregation, made her heart flutter.

After a light breakfast, Lily presented Connie with a wedding dress.

It wasn't a wedding dress in the traditional sense, but Lily described it as pure white and beautiful.

And even though at the time when Lily had purchased the dress she didn't know it, but it was a dress that was meant for Connie McGreevy.

It was times like this that Connie missed her vision the most. But she was quickly reminded how blessed she was when she heard Florence's little voice laughing merrily as she played in the parlor with her new friend Uncle Thaddeus, and her new toys.

Connie was happy and relieved by how easily Florence settled in for the night with them. She accepted Connie and Sam as her new mama and papa without question.

It was that simple.

As soon as the couple was escorted into the church, Lily's sister, Rosey Larsen took charge of Florence.

The vicar's wife presented Connie with a bouquet.

"White roses," she said.

"Thank you, thank you so much," Connie said sincerely.

Finally, Lily fluffed Connie's dress and walked her to the front of the congregation where Sam waited with Thaddeus.

After the first half of the mass, Vicar Clausen called for Sam and Connie to approach the altar to affirm their vows before the congregation of witnesses.

Somehow, Sam managed to procure a wedding ring for Connie that he slipped onto her finger after he said his vows to Connie. She in turn said her vows to him, and Vicar Clausen affirmed their marriage under the eyes of God.

***

Christmas Day

After an indulgent lunch at the home of Thaddeus Anderton, the carriage was loaded with Florence's toys and clothing.

The carriage driver would collect Sam and Connie's possessions from The Albion and deliver them to the blind academy.

They finally said goodbye to Thaddeus and Lily and thanked them for their extreme generosity, their kindness, and their friendship.

Before Thaddeus closed the door to the carriage, he passed

two envelopes to Sam.

"What is it?" Connie asked as she settled Florence between them on the carriage.

Sam opened the first envelope. He was stunned.

"It's bank checks written out to the blind academy. Thaddeus, Doctor Scopes, Vicar Clausen, Judge Tavish, Doctor and Missus Larsen...well, everyone we met."

"How incredibly generous," Connie said.

"Yes, so very generous. This money will do so much good for the students, the staff, and the facilities."

"What is the other envelope?" Connie asked.

"The front of the envelope is written to Doctor and Missus McGreevy and daughter Miss Florence McGreevy."

Just saying their names out loud caused a huge surge of pride to fill his chest.

His family.

"Oh my goodness..."

"What is it, Sam?"

He heard the concern in Connie's voice.

"Nothing terrible, my darling, it is a bank check from Thaddeus and Lily, a very generous gift to start our lives out on sturdy footing."

Sam could hear the slight quiver in his voice.

The bank check was beyond generous.

Thaddeus Anderton was truly an exemplary man.

Miss Lily Rydall was an incredible upstanding woman.

When the couple finally married, and Sam was certain they would, Thaddeus and Lily would become the most powerful couple on Carlyle Street.

And deservingly so.

Once at the blind academy, Sam assumed his new posture

with his wife on one arm and his daughter carried in his other arm. Already it felt natural. Mister and Missus Caldwell greeted the family of three.

Florence's bags were sent to the cottage. The same would happen when the carriage arrived later in the day with Sam and Connie's possessions from the hotel.

"The children are waiting for your arrival inside," Missus Caldwell said. "We are so incredibly grateful to you both for not only joining us at the academy to teach and doctor, respectively, but for the donations of toys and clothing for the children, and the food parcels from both yourselves and Doctor Scopes."

"We also have these donations to pass along from our friends," Sam said passing the envelope of bank checks to Missus Caldwell.

Mister Caldwell looked over his wife's shoulder as she opened the envelope. Immediately, her hand went to her heart.

"There is much goodness still in the world," Mister Caldwell stated.

"Yes Sir, there certainly is," Sam said sincerely.

After the Caldwell's went back inside the main building, Sam, Connie, and Florence lagged behind.

"Well, my beautiful girls, are you both ready to begin our lives together?" Sam asked.

"Yes, absolutely," Connie said.

"Yes, Papa," Florence said in her most adorable voice.

Sam had to clear the emotion from his throat.

He pressed a kiss against Florence's brow, and a gentle kiss to Connie's lips.

"I love you both so much," he said.

"I love you, Sam, and I love you, Florence," Connie said with a smile on her lips.

It was a glorious smile.

"I love you, Mama," Florence said happily.

Sam straightened his shoulders and walked his little family into the academy to celebrate Christmas with the children.

This was where he belonged.

He was a blessed man.

Chapter 15

E *pilogue*
January 1893

Transcribed into writing by Sam.

Dearest Auntie Minerva,

I must first apologize for the lateness of this letter.

Things have been so busy since I arrived at The Carlyle Academy for the Blind.

Yes, what was once the blind asylum, and then the blind academy now is known as The Carlyle Academy for the Blind. It's much nicer, don't you agree?

Sam, Florence, and I are looking forward to visiting this spring.

I cannot wait for you to meet my little family!

Auntie Minerva, you were so very right about Carlyle Street being magical. As soon as I arrived at Carlyle Street and The Albion Hotel that cold early December night and met Sam, my life changed for the better. I knew immediately that I had met my future husband.

And then we were blessed with Florence entering our life.

We needed Florence as much as she needed us.

She accepted us as her mama and papa without hesitation. She is the light of our lives. We love her so much.

Sam has settled into the medical facilities at the academy and is attending to the medical needs of the students. I am enjoying teaching music to the students and they are so eager to learn. Florence is so happy to be with me during study hours. At the end of the day, Sam collects us and we return to our darling little cottage on the academy grounds.

I even received good news from Doctor Scopes that his recently blinded niece, Sophie, has agreed to spend a few hours a week at the academy alongside me. I prayed for this, and God heard my prayers. I have been so worried for Sophie. I hope this step she is taking will lead her in the right direction to become a fully functioning, confident blind woman.

Well, my Dearest Auntie, I will close here but will write again soon. I cannot wait to see you and the family again this spring.

I look forward to your next letter.

With Love,

Your niece, Constance

About the Author

Natalie-Nicole Bates has worn all the hats in the publishing world – reader, reviewer, author, and now small publisher. She has the ability to see the point of view of everyone involved with the love of books.

With a taste for the darker side, Natalie-Nicole's favorite genres are Dark Victorian, Steampunk, and Dark Paranormal. Her interests include collecting Victorian-era photographs, Frozen Charlotte Dolls (her latest batch was just delivered from a German excavation site after being buried underground since about 1860), and antique poison bottles. She loves exploring and photographing cemeteries – the older, the better!

She makes her home in a rural little village in England.

You can connect with me on:

- https://www.natalienicolebates.com
- https://www.twitter.com/BatesNatalie
- https://www.facebooks.com/NNBates
- https://www.instagram.com/natalienicolebates
- https://www.facebook.com/groups/Natalienicolesnation

Also by Natalie-Nicole Bates

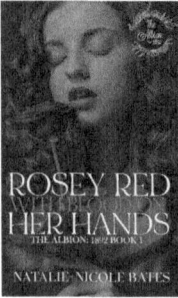

ROSEY RED WITH BLOOD ON HER HANDS : The Albion 1892 (Book 1)

The year is 1892. Rosey Rydall is a fiercely independent and entrepreneurial woman of the time.

Check-in girl at The Albion Hotel is only one of her jobs. In the background, she runs an informal body selling business with the town coroner, Anton Larsen. She also is a trusted friend and confidante of wealthy hotel mogul, Thaddeus Anderton. A friendship that is both loving and beneficial for Rosey.

Two men love Rosey.

She haunts the dreams and existence of Marty Burke, a much married, decorated, and respected police officer who looks the other way from Rosey's business, as well as the nighttime activities occurring in the basement of The Albion.

The other is her partner in crime, Doctor Anton Larsen, a man of true quality who loves the dark and dangerous as much as Rosey.

When Marty's wife dies, and he turns his attention to Rosey, she spurns his attempts at possessing her. In turn, he threatens everything and everyone Rosey loves. She must now take bold and decisive action to rid herself of Marty or risk the lives of those who mean the most to her.

HIS REDEMPTION : THE ALBION 1892 (Book 3)

With a baby on the way, it should have been the best Christmas ever for Evie Stanton. Instead, she finds herself a widow, and alone in a strange town. Luck seems to shine on Evie when she meets police officer Marty Burke. Marty is everything her late husband was not – kind, caring, and loyal. Marty offers to marry her, and give her and her baby a home.

It's almost too perfect until Evie hears rumors about Marty's past.

She finds it impossible to reconcile the handsome, wonderful man she knows, with the dark and dangerous man she is told about.

For Evie, her choice becomes one of uncertainty. Marry a man with a questionable reputation, or find herself homeless with a new baby.

DARKLY SKEWED : Dark Carnival (Book 1)

One night forever changed the life of Shaun Collins.

Once a successful and respected coroner, Shaun encountered a demon who rendered him nothing more than a living corpse, doomed to live on forever and ever.

And then Shaun found Dark Carnival.

A mysterious traveling curiosity show where all the performers have secrets. Assuming the persona of a clown, Shaun travels city to city, hating himself a bit more with each passing day.

Everything changes when he meets the most beautiful woman named Kyrie, who doesn't see what others see.

But to love Kyrie is not only selfish but dangerous as well.

Can Shaun find a way in his impossible world to keep the woman he loves, and return to a normal life once again, or will his desires destroy them both?

Printed in Great Britain
by Amazon

39564761R00086